Premier Amour
First Love

Hailing from the advertising industry, **Abhay** is educated as a visual designer and practised art direction for many years before picking up the pen full-time. Today, he writes for digital marketing and various digital transformation causes, brand communication and thought leadership communication. His work spans the North American, Asian, Southeast Asian and Middle Eastern and North African (MENA) markets.

Meanwhile, his pursuit of creative writing continues unabated.

When asked about himself, Abhay simply says that he is 'a storyteller with bandwidth'.

Abhay was closely associated with the drafting, editing and compiling of two books, *The Enlightened Entrepreneur* (2013) and *She & Me* (2014), written by the late Dr Bhavarlal H. Jain, a Padma Shri awardee and founder and former chairman of Jain Irrigation Systems Limited. Both these works are Rupa Publications' titles.

Abhay is an avid photographer and his subjects include, travel, street, culture, heritage and people.

You can find Abhay on Facebook at AforAbhay and on Twitter @agoghari.

Premier Amour: First Love is Abhay's debut novel.

Praise for the Book

This love story touches the heart, keeps coming back at you. The storytelling is evocative and engaging. The backdrop of the Zanskar valley adds a beautiful hue to this tale of first love. Don't just read this book. Savour it.

—**Sonal Dabral**, Ad guru

The emotions are very real. The imagery is vivid, and the narrative compelling. Every soul who has loved will relate to this love story.

—**Pan Nalin**, Film director, producer, screenwriter and editor

I love Zanskar, and I loved this *Zanskari* love story. It evolves so beautifully from the lap of the lofty mountains and then goes places, spreading strong messages along the way. The narrative is very touching throughout. Lovebirds, you have a new getaway—Zanskar.

—**Sandhya Chandrasekharayya**, Co-founder of Indiahikes

Premier Amour: First Love is a rare book—a well-written contemporary YA romance. The lead pair has well-sketched characters. Both Bhanu and Bhushan are endearing and realistic. This one is a keeper for the next vacation flight you take! Fun, intense and everything in-between.

—**Ilina Singh**, a restless multitalented student and aspiring scientific entrepreneur, receiver of Prime Minister's recognition for her creative expressions

Abhay's writing conjures a beautiful picture of the quintessential couple in love amidst snow-clad mountains. *Premier Amour: First Love* is fast-paced, fun and the perfect book for an afternoon in the sun.

> —**Anamika Sirohi**, Vice President of Marketing, Nutrition and Wellness and Community at Amway India

A breath of fresh air! The narrative, the imagery and the full range of emotions feel so freshly conjured and is written with a lot of soul in it. I actively engage with the youth, and I can sense this novel will resonate with them. It has what the Gen-Z wants and needs—A DIY on getting it right with love.

> —**Ambika Sharma**, Founder, Managing Director and Chief Strategist at Pulp Strategy Communications

I loved reading the draft as a beta reader; now I can't wait to own the novel!

> —**Harsh Patel**, student and service staff at a famous coffee shop, Toronto

This is love as it should be. Some pages grew on me as I read them again and again. They actually helped me nurture my marriage. There are 11 bookmarks I have placed between these pages!

> —**Vaishnavi Bhatt**, Jewellery Designer, Prague

Premier Amour
First Love

Abhay

RUPA

Published by
Rupa Publications India Pvt. Ltd 2022
7/16, Ansari Road, Daryaganj
New Delhi 110002

Sales centres:
Allahabad Bengaluru Chennai
Hyderabad Jaipur Kathmandu
Kolkata Mumbai

Copyright © Abhay Goghari 2022

All rights reserved.

No part of this publication may be reproduced, transmitted,
or stored in a retrieval system, in any form or by any means,
electronic, mechanical, photocopying, recording or otherwise,
without the prior permission of the publisher.

This is a work of fiction. Names, characters, places and incidents are either the
product of the author's imagination or are used fictitiously and any resemblance
to any actual person, living or dead, events or locales is entirely coincidental.

ISBN: 978-93-5520-338-0

First impression 2022

10 9 8 7 6 5 4 3 2 1

The moral right of the author has been asserted.

Printed at Thomson Press India Ltd., Faridabad

This book is sold subject to the condition that it shall not, by way
of trade or otherwise, be lent, resold, hired out, or otherwise circulated,
without the publisher's prior consent, in any form of binding or
cover other than that in which it is published.

*Every day, young hearts experience the ecstasy
or agony of falling or failing in love.
But love never fails us.
We fail love.*

∽

Contents

Author's Note	xi
Where It All Began	1

Part 1: Falling in Love

1. Tea Meets Tequila	5
2. Friendship Leads to Fondness, and the L Word Rolls Out	22
3. Cloud Nine Comes Crashing Down	40

Part 2: Failing in Love

4. It Hurts Badly To Fail in Love	47
5. Mother's Love Helps To Get Over Other Love	80
6. The Hurt Heart Begins To Heal	92
7. Tragedy Strikes Suddenly	107
8. Life After Loss and More Twists and Turns	122
9. Separation Is the Lesser Evil	129
10. New Beginnings	141
11. A Second Chance at First Love	146

12. The Stage Is Set for the Reunion	151

Part 3: Rising in Love

13. A Face-Off That Changes Everything	155
14. It's All Falling Into Place	167
15. The Forever Journey Begins	178
16. The End Is a New Beginning	216
Epilogue	222
A Parting Note	224
Gratitude	227

Author's Note

I tried many times to name the characters of mothers, but nothing came close to Mother. So I have let mothers be mothers.

Where It All Began

The Chadar Trek on the frozen River Zanskar

The Zanskar Valley in the northwestern Himalayas is part of the Kargil region in the union territory of Ladakh. It is one of the remotest and most inhospitable high-altitude valleys in the world. The entire area of 7,000 square kilometres supports a population of around 14,000 natives, comprising mostly of Tibetan Buddhists. The valley remains cut off from the rest of the world for most of the year due to heavy perennial snowfall. The average maximum winter temperature in Zanskar is -10°C. The only way to connect with the outer world during the long winters is to walk for six to seven days on the frozen Zanskar River in order to reach Leh. The journey on the harsh, frozen terrain is a supreme test even for the able-bodied and strong willed. High-altitude trekkers and climbers have found an irresistible challenge in this winter activity that is aptly called the Chadar Trek—a walk on the ice sheet.

Bhanu and Bhushan fall in love during their Chadar Trek. It is their first love—*premier amour*. Having evolved in the hardy ecology of Zanskar, it has to pass through many trials before it can qualify as lasting true love.

Part 1

Falling in Love

1

Tea Meets Tequila

First love. It is a maiden voyage through an uncharted course in the quest for a mysterious utopia. The stakes are high—very high. Yet, for those in love, the journey is worth its price. Ask the debutants, Bhushan and Bhanu. They will vouch for it.

～

Bhushan Bhanu Pratap Singh. Rich, pampered, arguably classy and fatally handsome. Age 24, hailing from Greater Kailash II, New Delhi.

He is the only child of a North Indian couple that has been through bad times before gaining affluence. His father, Bhanu Pratap Singh owns a popular upmarket chain of garment stores. Once bankrupt, he is now Delhi's leading clothing retailer. The couple's mutual obsession is to offer their son his life on a silver platter—of what use is their sweat and toil otherwise, they reason. Naturally, Bhushan has been subjected to a constant overdose of parental indulgence since he was a child. Girls are constantly in awe of his Bollywood-ready 6'1" frame. With a rich mane of stylishly unruly, dark brown hair, same-coloured deep-set eyes, dimpled right cheek, long legs; he is an irresistible package. His branded lifestyle and penchant for extravagance add to his aura of awesomeness. His popularity easily made up for his average academic record when he was in college. He used to joke that one could either be studious or a stud—to each their own.

However, despite being hoity-toity and a bit of a show-off, Bhushan is a habitual do-gooder; he is large-hearted and kind. Spoilt he may be, immoral he is not.

Although he is not single, he has never been in love. He is struck by love only when he meets Bhanu.

Ah, Bhanu, our fair lady, the only child of Mrs and Dr Gajendra Prasad Bhutia, who hail from Gangtok but have been living in Mumbai for three decades. Bhanu is a confident, young woman with a weakness for brains rather than brawn—the polar opposite of Bhushan.

She is of above-average height and looks, has a broad forehead and teeth like pearls in a necklace. She is 'mole-girl' for friends, thanks to a prominent, walnut-brown mole sitting pretty on her upper lip. By far, her most striking features are her naturally straight, silky, black hair and flawless, creamy complexion with supple skin that blushes when pinched. And she has a sweet, lingeringly sonorous voice that sounds like the tinkling of a copper wind-chime hung high on a tree.

Bhanu's parents are consummate academicians. Mrs Bhutia began her career as a substitute teacher in a missionary school, and over time, became the principal. She advocates for social and women's causes. On the other hand, Dr Bhutia emerged as a renowned historian sought after by national and international universities.

The Bhutia family lives comfortably but not with excesses. In place of affluence, they have earned tremendous respect from the intelligentsia and the academic fraternity.

Having grown up in a liberal atmosphere, Bhanu is a free-willed person with a mind of her own. And she uses it liberally on unsuitable boys making advances at her.

At 21, Bhanu is single and waiting for her brainy knight in a thinking cap. Bhanu and Bhushan were like tea and tequila. Until they met in Zanskar.

~

Bhushan learned about the Chadar Trek on a hot May afternoon as he was killing time in his father's plush, air-conditioned office, apparently minding the business. Delhi was roasting. The heat wave slapped you hard the moment you stepped out on to the streets. People scrambled for the hill stations and summer treks to cooler places. Fed up with Delhi, Bhushan googled 'fun adventure treks in the Himalayas,' and Google returned more than 19 lakh results in 0.2 seconds. The third ad caught Bhushan's eyes; it was not a summer trek but a winter adventure. 'Trekking in the Himalayas in the winter? Come on, Google, don't take me so seriously,' he joked to himself, 'I'm just looking for an escape from the scorching Delhi heat and some fun and thrills to boast about to the girls when I return.' However, curiosity got the better of him and he clicked on the ad. The landing page read,

> Go where a few dare to go. Walk on the frozen Zanskar
> River for 7 days in -20°C. Have you got it in you?

Bhushan's ego was challenged. He probed further. The panoramic snowscapes that opened up before him were breathtaking. Tiny figures of trekkers clad in layers of warm clothing looked like penguins captured with a wide-angle lens. The river had both fluid and icy avatars, with snow banks on both sides. And the towering blue-white mountains looked ethereal, almost like sci-fi props.

Even before he read the details, Bhushan knew he had to go on this trek.

He called up a friend who had a friend who knew a Himalayan trek organizer. Yes, the Chadar Trek was for real. And yes, they had three vacancies. Bhushan immediately registered on the website.

The trek's difficulty level was classified as 'challenging,' which meant that it required a high level of physical and mental fitness. Bhushan thought, *what the heck, I will have something to do after all.*

In Mumbai, Bhanu, too, was fed up with the heat and the rising humidity. Although the temperature hovered around 39°C, it felt 42-ish. Even air-conditioned metro travel turned sticky and sweaty after a while. Bhanu ventured out only in the respite of evenings to hang out with her friends.

One such evening, she told her friend Freny, from Goa, whom she had aptly nicknamed Feni, 'Phewww Feni, I want to escape to the Himalayas.'

'Taking sanyaas or what?'

'Whatever yaar, I need a break from Mumbai's May.'

'Tathaastu [So be it],' Feni said and opened the browser on her phone.

She googled 'summer treks in North India' and handed her phone to Bhanu. The second ad caught her attention, 'The Chadar Trek—A majestic and menacing winter Himalayan experience.'

Bhanu had experienced snowfall in Gangtok, her ancestral town, and made snowmen and thrown snowballs at her friends when she was a child. But to walk on a goddamn frozen river for seven days like a lost snow hare! That sounded like serious stuff.

'This is epic shit, yaar,' Bhanu told Feni.

'Let's do it then!' the adventurous Feni exclaimed.

'Yo!' they high-fived in instant agreement.

Once home, Bhanu told her parents about the trek. They looked wary.

'Why not, maa, Paa?'

'It's too risky,' Dr Bhutia said.

'Come on, Paa, ceilings of well-built homes collapse at night in Mumbai, and people die in their sleep.'

'It requires advanced levels of fitness and endurance,' Mrs Bhutia said in her husband's defence.

Bhanu shot back, 'I can achieve that.'

Maa taunted, 'You don't get up before noon, and your last three New Year's resolutions have gone for a toss.'

'Lol. Tomorrow onwards I will get up early and help you in the kitchen as well,' Bhanu pestered.

'Ha!' Mother mocked, 'Jokes apart, even if we agree, will you go alone?'

'Feni is coming.'

Her parents' expressions hinted at vague leniency, and they ended the discussion by telling her that they would think about it.

But to Bhanu's bad luck, Feni's resolve had fizzled out by the next evening.

'Shit, yaar! What happened?' Bhanu complained.

'Parents happened. They won't allow me.'

'Shit!'

'Yeah, shit happens,' Feni mumbled indifferently, giving more importance to chewing gum than listening to Bhanu.

Bhanu felt deserted and let down. Her parents now had a strong reason not to let her go. But she was a genius at playing them on a sticky wicket. She would try to appeal to her mother's sense of social justice and lace her proposal with a liberal amount of feminist pride and emotion, and as a last resort, she would turn to hurt and dismay.

'Maa, Paa, Indian women in recent times, have gone as far as Antarctica and closer home they have scaled Mt Everest multiple times. Do you think they are any less than men? By denying me this adventure, you are in fact showing gender bias.'

'It's not like that Bhanu...,' Dr Bhutia said, but she interrupted him, 'Oh come on, Paa, would you have stopped me from going if I were your son?'

That had an immediate effect on her mother. In fifteen seconds, Bhanu had raised three issues very close to her mother's heart. Maa was touched.

'You are right, Bhanu, but we are right too, in worrying for you.'

Bhanu knew that if she could melt her mother, her job was done. She made a frontal attack,

'Maa, you always say you treat me just as you would your son but when the chance comes to prove it, you back out.' With that, she sulked in her chair, wearing a disappointed look.

'It's a challenging trek, and that's why we are worried. You have never done such a rigorous trek.'

'How could I, if you don't let me?' Bhanu straightened in her chair and looked at mother.

'What if something happens to you...?'

Bhanu timed it perfectly. She got up and stormed out of the room, stamping her feet in anger.

'Wait, Bhanu.'

'No point, you've already decided not to let me go.'

'What about dinner?' Mother asked.

'I'm not hungry,' Bhanu said and slammed the door of her room.

Ten minutes later, Bhanu heard Mother's soft knock on her door, 'Bhanu?'

'What now?'

'Dinner is getting cold.'

'I told you, I'm not hungry.'

'Okay, your father and I have discussed it. We are okay if you would still like to go.'

Bhanu rushed out and wrapped her parents in a bear hug.

'Love you, maa and Paa, thank you sooo muchhhh!'

She suddenly found her appetite.

~

By January, Bhanu was ready for Zanskar. She could jog for ten kilometres, climb ten storeys taking two steps at a time, and skip for fifteen minutes without getting breathless. On the day she left for the trek, Dr Bhutia joked at the airport, 'Snow time, beta.'

'Showtime, Paa,' she replied and hugged him.

Her mother's face clouded a bit, and Bhanu scolded her mildly, 'Maa! It's not my bidaai.'

Mother took Bhanu in her arms and kissed her forehead, 'Be safe.'

'I will,' Bhanu assured her.

But that was not to be. Harm and hurt come in so many forms.

~

One of the trek organizers received Bhanu at the Delhi airport and led her to the youth hostel boarding house where the trekkers would be staying overnight. Apart from Bhanu, there was just one other girl in the group of ten—Richa, from Lucknow.

'Two is company,' Bhanu said when the organizer introduced them.

'Jolly good company!' The other girl replied, and they shook hands jovially.

Bhushan had joined the group an hour ago. He had expected at least half the group to be girls, but was disappointed to meet just one. He had asked the organizer, 'More members joining us?'

'One more from Mumbai. She's arriving shortly.'

'She!' Bhushan had heaved a sigh of relief.

Once Bhanu reached the boarding house and freshened up, she was introduced to the group.

'And this is Bhushan,' the organizer said as they approached him.

Bhushan straightened to capitalize on his 6'1" frame and then bowed slightly while extending his hand. He rolled out his full name in style, 'Bhushan Bhanu Pratap Singh. Pleasure is all mine, err…'

'Bhanu, just Bhanu.'

She avoided shaking his hand and joined her palms together in a sanskaari namaste.

'Bhanu! Lovely name. Nice to meet you, I am Bhushan Bhanu Pratap Singh,' he repeated his entire name.

'Won't you add your ancestors' names and introduce them too?' Bhanu breezed past him with a faint mocking smile.

That was a disaster, but Bhushan was determined not to give up easily. *Sometimes girls disguise their liking in dislike*, he consoled himself.

As they left for the airport the next morning, Bhushan offered to help Bhanu with her luggage.

'Hi Bhanu, good morning!' he said cheerfully and bent to pick up her two rucksacks, 'Allow me, please.'

Bhanu looked past him and called out to the boarding house's helping hand, 'Will you please help with my luggage?'

Bhushan gave her a perplexed look, 'Hello?'

Only then did she notice him, 'Oh hi!' she reciprocated and pretended to recollect his full name, 'Uuummm, Dushan Bhanu Pratap Singh, right?'

'Bhushan.'

'My bad! So sorry, Bhushan.'

'It's okay, Bhanu.'

Bhushan stuck with Bhanu so that he could secure a seat beside her in the Scorpio. Bhanu let him, and at the last moment called out to Richa, the only other girl in the group, 'Hey come here!' She patted the space beside her, 'Let's catch up on our way. So how is Lucknow? I've never been there…'

Inside the aircraft, however, Bhushan's wish was granted by a stroke of luck. They had adjoining seat numbers.

'My seat.' He told Bhanu, pointing at the window chair. Once settled, he started the conversation, 'So, you are from Mumbai?'

'Yes.'

'I am from Delhi.'

No response.

'Isn't Mumbai too congested and polluted?'

'Can't beat the smog of Delhi, though.'

'That's only during peak winter.'

'Congestion is only during peak traffic hours.'

This one is a tough nut to crack, but she will come around, keep trying, Bhushan tried to pump his depleting confidence. Changing track, he asked, 'Are you still a college student?'

'Appeared for graduation finals.'

'I graduated in Law. Now I work for my father's business. Your major?'

'Journalism.'

'Oh! Future Dutt!'

Bhanu made a face conveying a civilized disapproval of flattery and picked up the airline magazine. Bhushan would not court defeat so easily.

'Are you going on the Zanskar trek for the first time?'

'No, I invented this trek,' Bhanu snapped and buried her head in the magazine.

That was blunt and promptly silenced Bhushan. When breakfast was served, Bhanu thought of making up with him just a tad so that she would not come across as arrogant.

'Dushan, err, Bhushan, would you hold the tray for me, please? I need to take out medicine from my purse.'

Bhushan leapt to her help and hurt his elbow in the cramped seats of the economy class.

'Ouch!' he winced.

Bhanu smiled sympathetically. Taking back the tray from him, she said, 'Thanks. Actually, I hate airline food, especially breakfast. It's often recycled.'

'You can't be more right, Bhanu. It's so stale. I'm addicted to mom-made fresh breakfast.'

'Still a momma's boy?'

'Aahh! I'm a victim of my mother's spoils,' Bhushan leaned a little towards Bhanu and smiled his dimpled smile.

Bhanu decided that it was time to pull the plug, 'I hate it when adults lean on their parents. I would rather prepare breakfast for my Maa.'

Nothing was working out for Bhushan that morning. That is usually very depressing for rich, handsome guys who take it for granted that girls will like them instantly. He reclined in his seat and looked out at the sky. It was cloudless and still. After a while, he looked at Bhanu and said, 'Beautiful.'

'I am used to hearing that,' Bhanu turned into a snob.

'I meant the sky looks beautiful.'

'Oh, that. It's just an empty patch of blue. It's so pale and anaemic, very depressing.'

Bhushan tried to engage Bhanu a few more times, but she did not throw him a bone. This continued in Leh as well, where they were given one day to acclimatize and shop for necessities and souvenirs. Bhushan offered to take her out to the markets, but she did not respond. By noon, he was desperate for results. At the eatery where they were served lunch, he pounced on the seat opposite Bhanu and asked, 'May I?'

'You've already taken the seat.'

'Oh! I thought you wouldn't mind.'

'Suit yourself.'

He showed her an intricately carved metal gong and a few other things he had bought. It was all very beautiful, and Bhanu liked everything he showed her, but she continued to play hard-to-get, 'Very common stuff, I hope you don't mind.'

She ordered a salad along with her favourite, momos.

'Weight-watching or what?' he asked.

'Never needed to. I'm not addicted to mom-made breakfast naa, that's why.'

Silence followed. Bhushan realized that he was running out of things to say, so he began to dish out Whatsapp jokes, 'While you relish your salad, here's a cute PJ: why did the tomato blush?'

Bhanu looked at him impassively, so he finished it himself, 'Because it saw the salad dressing!'

With the other one, he did not wait for her to reply, 'How is your long-distance relationship going? So far, so good.'

'Funny, no?'

'Yeah, I did laugh at it when I heard it for the first time.'

After a while, Bhushan was desperate to the point of being direct. He blurted, 'Are you single?'

And Bhanu cringed. Looking up from her salad, she snapped, 'Now look here, dude, my being single or not is none of your business. I am tolerating you out of civility and the fact that we are in the same group. Else, please know that we are like chalk and cheese.'

That was like pouring water on both—chalk turned into a soggy lump and the slice of cheese was a sticky mess.

~

The group gathered for a preparatory briefing after dinner.

'So, is everybody fighting fit?' the organizer's question was greeted with an energetic chorus, 'Yeah!'

'Great! So here are a few dos and don'ts to make your Zanskar experience safe and enjoyable. First of all, remember that your lower half is your better half!' After some laughs from the group, he continued, 'Seriously, you must remain dry—very dry—during the trek. And for that, gumboots are your best bet. Also, keep a few pairs of woollen socks handy. Next, wear four or five layers of clothing topped by a waterproof windcheater instead of wearing one or two thick woollens.'

'Why so?' Richa asked.

'Simple, layers are barriers. So, fortify your body against the bone-chilling cold with multiple barriers. Also, wear dark, anti-glare biker's sunglasses. And guys, point-and-shoot cameras are better than high-tech DSLRs, which often don't function well in such brutally cold conditions. They don't serve any purpose other than an added weight to your backpack. And that brings me to a very important point—travel light because the air is going to be thin and you'll be breathless very easily. Now, how to avoid hypothermia? Don't expose your face, neck, fingers, etc., to the cold, as you will lose body heat through the skin's pores. Remember, your body is the only heater you have in Zanskar. This is a challenging trek, so you must preserve and use your energy very judiciously. Walk at a steady pace, and please, guys, walk with caution. The ice is unstable and unreliable. Avoid cracked surfaces, and if the ice cracks after you've stepped on it, quickly switch to a different patch that looks solid. It is equally important to avoid slippery patches. Above all, don't panic under any situation.'

'What about food?' mom-fed Bhushan asked.

The organizer chuckled, 'Don't worry, Bhushan, we will feed you properly. But don't expect regular meals. We'll have noodles, chhole-puri, and such stuff. You'll be treated to gulab jamuns a few times, as well. And I'm sure all of you would have brought energy snacks, as recommended in our brochure.'

Wrapping up his talk, the organizer asked, 'Any questions?'

The group had none.

'All right then, the wake-up call is at 5:00 a.m.'

~

The group was raring to go around 7:00 a.m. Three cabs waited to take them to Tilad Do via Chilling, where the adventure began. The trekkers had heard about the rugged drive, especially around Nimu village, where they would witness the confluence of the Zanskar and Indus Rivers. They were all perked up; the thrill was about to begin!

Since Bhushan was fond of motorcycles; he had opted to do the distance on a rented bike. The bike owner would ride as the pillion passenger and would return on his bike from Tilad Do.

The road was almost deserted. High, ochre-brown cliffs towered over it on both sides and tattered patches of snow covered the soil here and there. There was no vegetation of any kind; the desolate, barren beauty of the region was overpowering.

Bhushan had the road to himself. He showed off his talents and a few bike stunts, mostly to impress Bhanu. He zoomed past the cabs, slowed down, then again, overtook them, crisscrossed the cabs with his expert manoeuvres, and so on. Bhanu was too busy to notice him, playing Pat-a-Cake, Mary Mack, and other clapping games, or singing out loud or joking around.

They had a brief stopover at the confluence of Zanskar and Indus. The road was elevated, so they had an excellent view of the rivers meeting far below. It seemed as if an invisible magnet was pulling two azure streaks of water towards each other. When they met, they fused effortlessly. It was a wonderful spectacle. Bhanu looked for her camera in the rucksack and was aghast, 'Gosh, oh no! Oh nooo! How stupid of me! It seems that I've left my camera back at the hotel.'

She sulked and sat down, her head in her hands, 'How stupid of me, shittt!'

The other girl came to her, 'Now what?'

'No pics, that's what!'

Bhushan vroomed by just then, and Bhanu saw the solution to her problem in him.

'Hey, Bhushan, you are terrific at bike stunts. I was watching you all the while.'

The tough nut is cracking, he complimented himself. Aloud, he said, 'Am I? They're just a few tricks I learned on the college campus. Old habits die hard.'

'Yeah, yeah, trying to impress girls, I'm sure,' Bhanu pumped his ego, then added as an afterthought, 'Oh, by the way, Bhushan, I am struck by tragedy.'

'You mean, tragedy is struck by you?'

'Good one! But seriously, yaar, I forgot my camera in Leh. Now, what do I do?'

The 'yaar' thing worked, 'Oh no! But hey, Bhanu! I can take you back to Leh, and we can collect it in a jiffy. Don't worry.'

'Then let's hurry,' Bhanu sprang on her feet and dethroned the bike owner from the back seat.

Bhushan applied the brakes a few times, even on the empty road. But Bhanu knew such unexpected emergencies would occur, so she leaned back in her seat to preempt any untoward incidents. After a while, he gave up.

Bhanu's camera was waiting for her at the hotel's reception counter. On their return drive, they stopped at the Zanskar–Indus sangam, Bhanu took many photographs, and they caught up with the group at Chilling. By then, Bhanu knew Bhushan's life story and ancestral history. The drive also helped her know him up close—he was as good at heart as he was good-looking, had a helpful nature, was bubbly and witty, and could be fun to hang around with. Overall score, 3.5/5. She upped his ranking by a few notches from negative to neutral in her mind and summed up—definitely impressive and attractive to girls in general, and like wine, he could get better with time. But he was definitely not for her because he was too much on the showy side.

'I'm back with the camera!' She chirped as she joined the group, 'Let's celebrate with a groupfie.' And she clicked her first picture in Zanskar with the distant snow-clad cliffs in the background. To Bhushan, she said, 'Thank you sooo much,' and then immediately added, 'Hey, dude, let's click a selfie.'

It was a nice selfie. Lots of teeth showing, trek-time swag, energy overdose, the boy leaning toward the girl, her free arm resting on his shoulder, a friends-with-possibility-for-more selfie.

~

The possibility for more increased during the day. As if in a natural extension of their bike ride, Bhanu and Bhushan walked together, trailing behind the rest of the group. The bike ride had created a comfort zone between them. She thought, *I will have to give this to him; he can make a girl comfortable around him.* And so she told him about her family, her friends, her love for reading, her tendency to call a spade a spade and her natural dislike for showy guys. At that, Bhushan asked, 'Oh! Is that why you were avoiding me?'

'I still am.'

'Nice! Walk with a guy and tell him all about yourself if you want to avoid him.'

Bhanu liked his humour, and gave him a friendly wink.

Before they knew it, their comfort zone had turned into a fondness for each other. Bhanu began to like the way he matched her stride. He listened to her and gave her his undivided attention. She felt cared for, respected and protected. And by God, he looked handsome despite the layers of clothing. *Careful*, she nudged herself; *you might fall for him.*

For Bhushan, Bhanu was unlike any other girl he had met. Her confident demeanour, her couldn't-care-less and tit-for-tat attitude, attractive looks, effortless English, perfectly modulated, sweet voice, ready humour, quick interchange between naughty and serious, she was his dream girl.

By late evening, they were clicking each other's pictures without asking for permission. Cozy friendship was setting in and the usual formalities seemed unnecessary.

The call for dinner went out at around 7:00 p.m. Bhushan, carrying two plates of noodles, walked towards Bhanu. Despite all the preparatory training, the first day of the trek was hard on everybody. Bhanu was resting against a flat stone, with her rucksack tucked under her head like a pillow.

Bhushan handed her a plate, 'It's a four-course dinner. Noodles, noodles, noodles, and noodles.'

'Beggars can't be choosers,' Bhanu said as she took her plate greedily.

When they were done devouring noodles, Bhushan took out two energy bars from his backpack and handed her one, 'Sweet for dessert.'

Bhanu grabbed both the bars, 'One is not enough.'

Their bond was growing stronger with such tongue-in-cheek exchanges. Bhanu felt that she could be herself with him, without worrying about manners or etiquette.

༄

2

Friendship Leads to Fondness, and the L Word Rolls Out

By the next morning Bhushan had become 'Bhusy', just like Bhanu had turned her friend 'Freny' into 'Feni'. It had begun to snow and Bhushan's moustache caught a few snowflakes. Bhanu exclaimed, 'Hey look at your muchhi [moustache]!'

'Snow?'

'Yeah, it looks mushy,' and her nicknaming talent surfaced instantly, 'Mushy Bhushy.'

The name 'Bhushy' went viral in the group within minutes. In the next hour, Bhanu got a taste of her own nicknaming talent.

The river had suddenly lost the frozen top layer of ice. So the trekkers began to walk along the bank. Bhanu saw something reflect the sunlight brilliantly on the riverbank. It was a shiny, marble-textured teal pebble.

'Sexy!' she said as she bent to pick it up.

In a flash, Bhushan took a photograph of Bhanu; her hunched body covered with layers of woollens made her look like a baby bear.

'How do I look?' She asked.

'Like a bhalu.'

She laughed sweetly and arched her head, clawing her fingers and making an animal sound, 'Ggrrrrrr.'

The possibility for more seemed like a certainty now.

~

The Chadar continued to be treacherous and unpredictable on the next day. It was difficult to judge whether the ice would hold or give away under a trekker's weight. Bhanu stepped on one such patch and the ice cracked under her with a low crunch. She panicked. First, she felt as if a carpet was being pulled from under her feet. Then the feeling enlarged into something like a micro-earthquake. The ice patch began to wobble and she lost her balance twice.

'Help!' Bhanu screamed. Bhushan was within an arm's length; he yelled, 'Bhanu! Don't panic. It's all right. You're going to be fine. Stay calm and still.'

Bhanu looked down and saw a strong, swirling current of water flowing below the patch of ice on which she stood frozen. It could sweep a person along with it as if one were a twig. She looked up desperately at Bhushan with frightened, pleading eyes. He extended his hand and Bhanu reached out out to him desperately. Once Bhushan had a firm grip on Bhanu, he pulled her towards him with all his strength.

'Jump!' He said and Bhanu jumped. In a second, she was in his arms, and the now-familiar feeling of safety and protection engulfed her. The tragedy ended as quickly as it had begun.

The organizer rushed towards them, 'You okay, Bhanu?' He asked, but she was unable to speak. Sobs of relief escaped her mouth as she watched the patch of ice on which she stood mere moments ago, disintegrate and drift away in tiny shards that dissolved in the water in seconds. Bhushan held her tightly. Moments passed and she regained her composure, but was still unwilling to let go of Bhushan.

'Thanks, Bhushy.' she breathed softly into his neck.

Bhushy. This time around, it was more than a friendly nickname. In reply, he nudged her encouragingly and smiled his dimpled smile. In that moment, she fell for him.

After long moments, she released her hug and looked at him, 'You single?'

Bhushan remained silent, and Bhanu took it as a 'Yes'.

Relief ran through her body. Then, mischief seized her, 'You see? Timing is everything, dude. If you ask a girl that question over a bowl of salad, cabbage is what you get. Now try your luck again.'

He tried his luck again, 'You single, Bhanu?'

These words were music to her heart. She blushed, 'Maybe.'

The rest of the day was uneventful in comparison, except that invisible bagpipers continued to play in Bhanu's and Bhushan's ears.

~

By the fourth day of the trek, gossip and guesswork ran amok in the group.

'What do you think?'
'About what?'
'About Bhanu and Bhushan, yaar!'
'Well, it's obvious, isn't it?'
'Look how they are bonding.'
'Like Fevicol.'
'Yeah, right man, looks like his jugaad worked.'
'Specially after she slipped on the ice.'
'She's on a slippery wicket.'
'Something is definitely cooking.'

'I hope it's spicier than our bland and boring noodles.'
'Spicy and hot.'
'Damn, she is sexy. I hope Bhushan doesn't make it with her.'
When the matter finally came to the organizer and someone asked what he thought, he joked, 'Well, in all likelihood, yes, but let's wait for the official confirmation.'
They did not have to wait long.
As they rested after lunch, Bhanu took to doodling in her field diary. Bhushan asked, 'Hey, Picasso, wassup?'
Bhanu complained, 'At least compare me with a female artist.'
'Okay, hey, Picassi, wassup?'
She laughed out loud and showed him her doodle. It was a basic wireframe stick figure of a boy and a girl holding hands. She asked him, 'What happens when a flirt meets a snob?'
'They fall in love,' Bhushan replied simply.
So there it was, the L word, the formal acknowledgment.
A woman's heart in love is like a peacock in the rains. It has to give in to singing and dancing in joy, flutter its wet rainbow feathers and spread them in an oversized arch, then it has to strut all over the place wearing that colourful cloak, announcing to the world that thus begins, the season of love.
Bhanu's heart was on a song. Love had come calling. How could she not respond? Unexpectedly, she bent and gave him a quick, soft kiss. He gave her a dazed look and she took a step back, in disbelief at her own impulsiveness, a shy, silly, blushing smile covered her face ear to ear. It took a full minute for Bhushan to recover from the impact of the kiss. Putting his hand on Bhanu's heart like how a doctor places a stethoscope, he said, 'Madam, you're suffering from an incurable disease.'
'What is it called?' Bhanu played along, expressing mock shock.

'First love.'

She pretended to look crestfallen, and slowly asked, 'Any chance of a cure, doctor?'

Bhushan shook his head from side to side in fake regret, and their laughter was amplified by the towering mountains.

Then, shedding mischief, Bhanu took Bhushan's hands in hers and said, 'I want you in my life as my macho man.'

He squeezed her hands, 'Copy that. It's official now.'

Bhanu went into a reverie, as first love came calling. She tore off the doodled page and started folding it slowly, carefully, neatly, as if it were the most important task of her life, ensuring that the folded ends matched perfectly. She took her time doing so, letting the fact that she was in love, sink in. She cried a bit. Bhushan wiped her tears and licked his fingers. She looked at him from behind her misty eyes, just like a girl utterly in love looks adoringly at her guy. Not knowing what to do next, she took his hands in hers again, more possessively this time.

Bhushan felt the need to loosen her up, 'Oye, drama queen, enough, let's celebrate.'

He lifted her up and she wrapped her legs around his waist. And just as he thought she would bring her face down to kiss him, she arched back and spread out her hands and cried out, 'Wwwoooooooohhhhhhhoooooooo!'

The other trekkers were keenly watching the outcome of the drama from a distance. As soon as Bhanu let out her cry of triumph, they closed in and started cheering and hooting and backslapping Bhanu and Bhushan.

'Let's celebrate, guys!' the organizer called out.

They made do with lukewarm tea to celebrate.

The group stopped for the day at around six in the evening. Their camping site had an overhang of a natural cave above the riverbank. Bhanu and Richa, the girl from Lucknow were to sleep in the relatively warmer cave, but the organizer warned them that there had been reports of big cats roaming the terrain at night.

'You mean leopards?' Richa was petrified.

'Snow leopards' he replied.

Richa cringed, 'I don't want to end as a feast for the predators around here. I'll take the tent on the riverbank.'

The organizer looked at Bhanu, 'What say? Tents are for two. We can't allot a whole tent to you.'

Instantly, wicked vibes flew between Bhanu and Bhushan. They looked at each other; the organizer looked at them and then looked away, as if nothing had transpired between the three of them. Bhushan took it from there, 'I don't mind moving to Bhanu's tent if that makes her feel safe. Besides, the January night sky offers some mesmerising views from the cave.' He said with the seriousness of a professor of celestial constellations.

Bhanu pretended to be hesitant, 'Well okay, but no monkey business.'

That is how Bhanu and Bhushan started 'sleeping with each other,' as she would articulate a little later.

~

Once in the tent, both of them quickly slipped into their sleeping bags. Despite the protective clothing and the insulation of the sleeping bags, the cold penetrated their bones. Lying on their backs, they watched the sky through the translucent material of the tent. It was indeed magnificent; nothing like either of them had ever experienced. The stars seemed to hang low, just within arm's reach. Those lying on the ground would be tempted to reach out and pluck a handful of them. For long moments, they lay silent, taking in the wild, ethereal beauty. Then Bhanu shifted her gaze from the stars and made an abrupt demand on Bhushan, 'My macho man, pluck a handful of stars for me.'

'As if they are grapes hanging in my grandfather's orchard.'

'C'mon, it's every girl's right to make that impossible demand on the first night that she spends sleeping with her guy under the stars.'

'"Sleeping with each other" is technically incorrect,' Bhushan observed. In there, zipped into sleeping bags, even holding each other's hands was out of question.

However, Bhanu continued to tease him, 'No point in trying. You're a certified frigid guy.'

'As if you have fire under your belly. Pun intended.'

Bhanu gave out a low, husky laugh, the only sound that emanated from the 7,000 square kilometres of the desolate, divine Zanskar Valley.

Their chatter went on endlessly, and they drifted into a shallow slumber only around dawn. Bhushan had set the alarm for 6:00 a.m., so that they could wake up along with everyone else in the group. As they got out of their sleeping bags, they attempted a hug, but could feel nothing through the numerous layers of clothes between them. Bhanu said, 'Now I know why astronauts don't make babies in space.'

'Because it's not possible to make love in zero gravity,' Bhushan reasoned.

'Not so technical, it's simply because they will catch a cold if they take off their clothes.'

'Moral of the story—don't attempt to make babies when you have a cold?'

'Ha!'

Then Bhushan teased, 'Let's make out.'

'Fuck you.'

'Can't wait.'

'No, but I will not fuck you, I'm a good girl.'

'Since when?'

Some more giggles followed before they hugged and kissed a fond and loving good-morning kiss.

As they came out of the tent and joined the group on the riverbank, tea was being served. Tsering, the ever-smiling Zanskari guide greeted them with a jovial 'Juleyy,' meaning 'hello', and handed them their cups. They greeted him and sipped the tepid brew—not the best tea on earth, but anything vaguely warm was most welcome. Breakfast of chhole-puri followed, and everybody had multiple generous servings of the steaming hot, spicy chickpea curry along with the soft fried flatbreads. They had many exhausting kilometres ahead of them that day.

Around mid-morning, the trekkers saw four young mothers and their children walking towards them. They were singing a Ladakhi ballad and their bodies were swaying to the rhythm. Totally oblivious to the harsh conditions, they strolled on the slippery and perilous frozen sheet of ice as if they were on a walk in the park. Then they noticed the trekkers. Their singing stopped and their freckled faces broke into shy, conscious smiles.

One of the mothers had an infant clutching at her bosom, snugly tucked in a weathered, leather sling bag. The ladies did not have enough warm covering and their exposed skins resembled the cracked and parched soil that awaits the first showers of the season. The children's plight was no better. They were untidy and ragged; their faces were smeared with frozen nasal discharge.

Bhanu was quick to start a conversation with them. Tsering doubled as an interpreter.

'Juleyy, where do you come from and where are you going?'

'We are from a village up there,' one of the ladies pointed in a general southern direction.

'How big is your village?' Bhanu asked.

'Seventeen houses,' the lady replied. Population, or the lack of it, was measured in terms of dwellings and not dwellers.

'And where are you going?'

'We are going to leave our children at the government school in Leh.'

Bhanu's jaw dropped in disbelief. It was unfathomable to her that children pursued studies even under those impossible conditions. She asked, 'You mean they go to school?'

'Yes.'

'Don't the young ones get frostbite without sufficient protective clothing?'

The lady replied, 'The high mountains are our protective shields. We worship the snow and the winds. How can they harm us?'

The trekkers were taken aback by her reply. It was profound, yet so simply said. Even in extreme poverty, she seemed more secure than those covered by the best security that money could buy. She was simply not worried that the elements would harm her. Centuries of isolation and inadequacies had made these people what they were—one of the hardiest and happiest native people in the world.

As Bhushan mulled the Zanskari lady's words, he realized

that the echoes of the urban slogan, 'Education for all,' resonated in this frigid Himalayan hinterland. Unlike in Delhi or Mumbai where parents complained if the school bus did not come for a day, parents here took near-fatal risks to make sure that their children could access and benefit from elementary education. It was also gender equality in action. Women were equal to men here, in all the survival tactics.

Breaking out of his reverie after a while, Bhushan swore, 'WTF!'

Bhanu looked at him questioningly but did not say anything. He continued, 'It's incredible, Bhanu, while we do this trek for fun and adventure, these women do it out of sheer necessity, so that their progeny can read and write. They don't even have clothes that are warm enough; they could die before they reach Leh. And we? We feel small if we don't have a new collection of winter wear each season.'

Bhanu was loving it. She had not seen this side of Bhushan before.

He summed it up, 'I've learned an important life lesson today. I will be self-sufficient from now.'

Bhanu made light of it, 'You mean you'll work your ass off to earn your winter wear and perfumes and even your fancy gadgets?'

'Yup, I'll even earn my talk time.'

'Good boy. Promise me that you'll spend all of it on me.'

'Girls! Why did God create them to be so jealous?'

'Because God created boys so flirty.'

~

By the third night, the lovebirds were comfortable talking about anything—their adolescent crushes, their fantasies, how

Bhanu loved her grandpa and why Bhushan loathed his, why she thought it was best if babies, like marriages, were made in heaven and then airdropped on earth, whether India would become a superpower by 2070, how, after marriage, they would treat their respective parents-in-law with due respect and so on.

It was 11-ish when Bhanu asked Bhushan to sing a love song for her.

Bhushan said, 'Bhanu, my watch says 23:09:19. Even the ghosts of Zanskar would be asleep by now, and I certainly don't want to displease them.'

'You have the choice of displeasing me.'

'I will choose the first option then.'

'Wise guy. Now sing for me.'

If there was anything Bhushan was bad at, it was singing. As he began to sing a popular Bollywood love song, Bhanu burst out laughing mirthlessly.

'Oye, my gruffy boyfriend, you sound like a monkey with a microphone.'

Bhushan stopped singing abruptly but Bhanu did not stop laughing. Between breaths, she continued to pull his leg, 'Kudos! My monkey maestro, you put Tansen to shame, really. He could light lamps singing the Raag Deepak and bring rains singing Raag Megh Malhar but you could trigger an avalanche with your Raag Pahaadi.'

Bhushan was genuinely embarrassed. Realizing that she had gone overboard, Bhanu immediately mended things with a flying kiss and a wink, 'Just pulling your leg, darling.'

'Just a kiss, and that too the flying version?' a quickly-mended Bhushan questioned.

'Then?'

'You'll have to sing that song for me.'

So she sang for him, and Zanskar sat up and listened.

Bhushan was fascinated, 'How do you have such a sweet voice?'

'How do you have such good looks?'

After a while, they finally said their good-nights and gave each other twenty-one winks salutes before reluctantly turning their backs to each other.

~

When one is thickly in love, magic transcends their wakeful moments and continues to act during sleep. A million darting dreams fly in and out of their paradisiacal kingdom. Everything is perfect like the poets have painstakingly narrated over the ages. And since the law of gravity or other such mundane rules don't tie down lovers to reality, their dreams take wings and soar high. The earth below becomes an insignificant maze. Bathing in the moist scent of the clouds, their hearts are cleansed deeply and they can love unconditionally, without inhibition, without restrictions, without duality. Having risen so high and travelled so far from the worldly order created by man, they finally get transported to God's own country—Lovers' Paradise.

In Bhanu's dream, she and Bhushan were cruising happily on the back of a fluffy cloud when they noticed Lovers' Paradise from a distance. Even in the misty haze, it looked like a Disney prop. Immediately attracted to it, they decided to check it out. When they landed at the arched gateway, they read the sign, 'Welcome to Lovers' Paradise.' There were no ticket booths or security checks, so they just walked right past the gate. Inside, they saw castles and mansions and pretty little dwellings and clean, shaded avenues and charming, elegant couples walking hand-in-hand on cobbled pathways adorned by flowerbeds on both sides. Some couples were seated on benches by the riverfront; others were watching a love ballad performance at the amphitheatre. And yet others were idling on the terraced slopes of the waterfront or sharing warm, hearty moments at coffee shops.

Bhanu and Bhushan were smitten by the charm of that place and decided to spend some days there. Luckily, a couple had just vacated a log cabin with a lake view, so they found ready accommodation in this heavily-in-demand resort. Their stay turned into a dream vacation. Minutes merged into hours and days into nights, until they lost track of time.

However, Bhushan's watch screamed its alarm at six, disrupting Bhanu's dream. She reluctantly drifted to wakefulness, as if recovering from anaesthesia. The last thing she remembered of her dream was a farewell note from the CEO of Lovers' Paradise:

Dear Bhanu and Bhushan,

It was a pleasure having you in this Paradise. I hope it helped you unwind, detox, rejuvenate, replenish, etc. Above all, I hope your stay helped you both to discover more of each other—that was the purpose of the vacation, isn't it?

However, all dream vacations must end. There is a long waiting-list of lovebirds impatient to get into this paradise. I am sorry but you are to resume duty on earth with immediate effect.

Your one-way tickets are enclosed.

With affection,
Almighty A. Altruist
Founder and CEO, Lovers' Paradise, Inc.

'WTF,' Bhanu muttered through a donut-sized yawn as she got out of her bag.

Not getting the context of the three-letter greeting, Bhushan looked at her, 'WTF what?'

'Nothing,' Bhanu said sleepily and gave him a fond hug.

That's the thing about women. Even when deeply in love, they like to keep some emotions to themselves, for they are too sacred to be shared.

The trekkers completed about the ten kilometres of gruelling walk on the Chadar by the end of the day. At dinner, one of the organizers said, 'Guys, I have bad news and good news; the bad news first. We are near the end of the trek. As you know, this is a one-way trek. After tomorrow's walk and we will spend the night at Nerak village, and then we will be going back the same way to Leh. So make the most of tomorrow. Now, the good news—tomorrow we shall witness the twin wonders of Nerak, the ancient Nerak Bridge suspended high above the Zanskar River and the gigantic 50-feet-high Nerak icefall. And surprise! There is a satellite phone at Nerak village which offers access to the outer world after this wonderful off-the-grid experience.'

With that, the group retired for the day.

~

There was a grand breakfast of gulab jamuns and puri-bhaji the next morning. The group fed itself greedily on the puris and the tangy potato curry, before setting off for the day's trek. Tsering walked a short distance with Bhushan and Bhanu to inform them about the twin wonders of Nerak. Bhanu loved the sweet, broken English that he had picked up from years of serving the climbers and trekkers. His native dialect made it sweeter.

'Memshaab, this Nerak is a great miracle of nature.'

'Really? Tell us more, naa,' Bhanu pushed him for more.

'It has an old-old wood brihze which my father's father

helped in making. And the other miracle is a ishfall which is as zhiant as 500 feet.'

Bhanu knew Tsering had added an extra zero to the bridge's height, but she let him oversell Nerak and chatted with him along the way.

After he had left, the lovebirds resumed their banter. Bhanu fast-forwarded their lives a couple of decades and teased Bhushan, 'Just imagine how you'll look when you are middle-aged. According to my predictions, you will be an early diabetic if you remain in my sweet company. You will have lost about 60 per cent of the hair on your head and 60 per cent of the remaining 40 per cent will have turned grey.'

She touched Bhushan's throat and said, 'And this sexy adam's apple of yours, it will then make you look like you have a frog trapped in your food pipe. To make matters worse, your snoring will become louder by many decibels, and at night you'll sound as if a cacophonic jugalbandi is emanating from your nose and mouth. It will be so noisy that you'll be nominated for the Snorer of the Year award.'

Bhushan was loving it, 'Thanks for all the name and fame, but will you be able to handle a celebrity-snorer hubby?'

'It would be my privilege and that's not all—you will also have gained a lot of weight and acquired a matka shaped paunch. Our Babli will roll her toy car on it, while Bunty plays the tabla.'

'What about Sonu, Monu, Bablu and Monty? What will they use papa's paunch for?'

'Bhanu made a thumb-down sign, 'Rascal, you're not getting your volleyball team. Two of us and two of ours, that's it. Bunty will be a nanotechnologist and Babli will become a choreographer. Both will have your looks and my brains, and Babli will have my voice too.'

'Wow! Designer babies—made to order?'
And they laughed themselves silly.

~

One never wants to end memorable experiences, but before one realizes, the end is near.

As the day advanced, the trekkers became acutely aware that their adventure would end that day. Greed set in and they tried to stuff tons of Zanskar in their memory bags.

For the organizers, it was a familiar phenomenon. They had observed this 'last-day' syndrome amongst trekkers year after year, but instead of slowly growing indifferent, they had become more sensitive to the bond that was invariably created between Zanskar and its visitors. Anybody who has been a good teacher would know the organizers' feelings on that last day. This is how teachers who bid farewell to the senior class feel. Although, every year they bid farewell to a new group of students, every class holds a very special place in the teachers' hearts.

As the group approached Nerak, they could see strings of boisterous, colourful prayer flags fluttering against the sapphire sky in the distance. These flags usually have prayers, chants or spiritual symbols printed or drawn on them and are an inseparable element of all the Tibetan Buddhist places of worship. Tsering, once again, donned the cap of a guide and said to Bhanu, 'Memshaab, in Zhanshkar we call them "Dar Cho".' Then, fumbling with words, he explained its meaning, 'It meansh that the wind and the shnow and other thingzh in nature are our "Dar" or Gods, who give us "Cho" or their protecshion and bleshings.'

Bhanu pondered on what he had said and immediately connected it with what the young Zanskari mother had told them a few days ago. She interpreted the meaning in her mind—'Dar' means the powers that enhance life-giving forces, good fortune, health, progress and prosperity, and 'Cho' means the recipients of such divine blessings.

Pondering over it, she turned to Bhushan and Tsering and said, as if in a greeting, 'Dar Cho.'

'Dar Cho,' they replied promptly.

At Nerak, the trekkers could see rows upon rows of prayer flags run across both the sides of the bridge. Some were even tied under the bridge's belly. The adornment gave the bridge a festive, 'inaugural' look, like how bridges are decorated before being dedicated to cities. In reality, though, the bridge was an ancient, creaky, rickety wooden structure erected with locally available primitive means, methods and materials. The effort was totally manual, undertaken without the aid of any mechanical device whatsoever. The bridge had no beams or pillars for support; it was a suspended structure that joined two cliffs. Its base was made of wooden slats that were tied to a row of wooden logs running across the length of the bridge. Some slippers had come off and were dangling in the air, giving a very precarious feeling to the structure. It had no railing or any other kind of handhold, so if one fell off it, one would land with a loud thud on the hard ice of the river. The bridge was very narrow and weak; it could take the weight of only four persons at a time.

A short distance away from the Nerak Bridge, the gigantic Nerak icefall loomed over the trekkers. It had a foamy texture running throughout its façade, so it looked like a massive wall of frozen foam.

The group of trekkers took plenty of photos and videos against the backdrop of this natural wonder. Bhushan and Bhanu got many pictures clicked there. In one of them, she jumped on

Bhushan's back, wrapped her legs around his waist and made a silly face at the camera. In another one, they were punching each other. And the last one was a selfie with beaming smiles.

'To us, we are forever!' Bhanu said as she pined over the photographs. Then, she mused, 'Has it only been a few days since I've been in love? Feels like ages.' Her heart was on a song, her soul, on a high. She closed her eyes and let her emotions spread through her every atom. It felt divine, other-worldly. A few ecstatic moments passed before she came out of her reverie. Showing her favourite photograph to Bhushan, she said, 'The forever couple' and then nudged him hard, 'My bastard BF, I'm warning you—don't you ever ditch me.' Bhushan looked at her but did not reply. Thinking that he, too, was on cloud nine, she let silence prevail.

∽

3

Cloud Nine Comes Crashing Down

The group camped for the night in a flat clearing just above the riverbed. In the morning, as they assembled at the icefall after breakfast, the trekkers saw a man hastily crossing the bridge—he was the person who manned the satellite phone at Nerak village. When he was halfway across the bridge, he called out to the group with hands cupped around his mouth. The trekkers could not understand his language. Tsering treaded hastily toward the bridge and the group saw him in an animated conversation with the man on the bridge. Then, he rushed back to the trekkers. He looked very anxious. It was not possible for him to form long sentences in English, so he mixed it up with his accented Hindi, 'Bhushan sir, one madam call to you on shattelite fone. From Delhi. Very urzhent, she said. She ask you to call to her immezhietly. Nerak villazhe is one hour from here. You pleazhe reach there soon and call that madam.'

Then, he quickly added, 'Wait, sir, I am also coming, the way is very hard and risky.'

Bhushan was petrified. Obviously, there was some ominous development back in Delhi. Bhanu too got worried. She said, 'I am coming'

Bhushan replied curtly, 'Nope, you're not.'

'I am. I'm getting terrible vibes.'

'You heard me, Bhanu.'

'Don't boss me around. I'm coming.'

Bhushan sensed that it was a waste of time arguing further and threw up his hands in helpless resignation. The trio started immediately. Nerak was about an hour's rigorous walk away and Bhushan was in a terrible rush. Bhanu tripped twice trying to match his rapid stride but got on her feet instantly, fearing that Bhushan would force her to stay back, citing her inability to take the rigour.

The villagers had gathered in full strength to receive them with the customary welcome drink of tepid tea. In the icy dreariness of their winter life, this was high drama, one which they just had to be a part of. Besides, it was natural for them to be of help whenever and wherever possible.

Even as he sipped his tea, Bhushan sought out a clear space and dialled his home phone number from the satellite handset. No reply. A chill ran down his spine as a thousand terrible thoughts crossed his mind. His face was already ashen, drained of all colour. He tried the number again. This time, a young lady answered the call, 'Hello?'

Although Bhanu was standing at a few feet's distance, she could hear the female voice clearly. She instinctively moved a couple of steps closer to ensure that she did not miss any part of the conversation.

Bhushan replied in an impatient, edgy voice, without any preamble, 'Brinda, what happened?'

The lady, at the other end, blurted in despair, 'Bhush darling! Thank God! You called back! Where are you and how soon can you come back home? Papaji suffered a massive stroke last night and he had to be rushed to the intensive care unit.'

Then, she broke into uncontrollable sobs.

Bhushan was numb with shock. He was oblivious of his surroundings. He had even forgotten that Bhanu was within earshot. He said, 'What are you saying, Brinda? Dad was hale and hearty when I left. Tell me what happened.'

Gathering herself up, Brinda said, 'Mummyji had called me over for the weekend to give them company. Papaji was okay when he went to sleep at eleven, but in the morning when Mummyji tried to wake him up, he did not recognize her. His face was crooked and he could not mouth the words properly. The left side of his entire body was paralyzed.'

Between sobs, she continued, 'Papaji's condition is very critical. Doctors have refused to say anything for the next 72 hours. I… err, we need you here, sweetheart. Come home as soon as possible.'

She was incapable of talking further. Bhushan ended the call abruptly, saying, 'All right.'

He then turned around and saw Bhanu standing at a few feet's distance. He tried in vain not to seem surprised at seeing her. His effort was clumsy.

'Who was she?' Bhanu's voice sounded steely, apparently devoid of all emotion.

Bhushan did not answer for a moment. Then, in a feeble, guilt-ridden voice, he said, 'Look, Bhanu…'

'Who is she?' Bhanu reframed the question, using the present tense. Her voice was laced with contempt, anger and anguish. It was the voice of a righteous woman who had found out that she had been cheated knowingly by the man she had trusted with her first love.

After a long pause, Bhushan replied, 'My fiancée.'

Bhanu did not react immediately. She was a strong-willed, assertive and self-assured woman who thought that she knew what she was getting into before she committed herself to that relationship. That is why the betrayal weighed heavily on her. Where did she go wrong? What was her fault? Even in a state of disorientation, she posed a flurry of questions to herself. The answers all came back to her in the negative; she was an innocent victim. This realization made her hate Bhushan all of a sudden.

If eyes could spew deadly venom and dart flares of pure hatred, Bhanu's eyes would've killed Bhushan. When she spoke finally she found herself spewing pure rage, 'You bastard! I told you not to betray me, didn't I?'

Even as she spoke, her voice cracked under the overwhelming weight of her hatred. She resumed in a low, gruff voice, 'I thought you were different, and that was the reason why I loved you. But you are one of them, a sly manipulative bastard. And anyways, I am the one to win my man, not steal him from another woman'

Despite everything, Bhanu did not cry. Either she was too proud to be seen as weak in front of others, or it was not like her to concede defeat to a coward, or she thought that he did not deserve her tears, or simply because her heart had already bled so much that her eyes could not cry—whatever be her reason, Bhanu did not cry. She did think of slapping him, but then immediately dismissed it as an understatement of her outrage. Instead, she did something that even she would have thought grossly unthinkable under any other circumstance—she spat on Bhushan's face, turned around and walked out of his life.

Part 2

Failing in Love

4

It Hurts Badly To Fail in Love

Surrounded by the prying village people, all Bhanu wanted at that point of time was to run away and never look back. But the moment the thought occurred to her, she realized that she had nowhere to go. Had this happened to her anywhere else, she would have caught the next train or flight back home. But she was in Zanskar, in the middle of nowhere. Let alone the idea of escaping from the depths of the icy valley; she could not even think of going back to the campsite on her own. Emotionally too, she felt trapped. Being who she was, righteous and self-respecting, she did not drown herself in self-pity. She did not think that that was the end of the road for her, even for a moment. At the same time, she felt utterly lost and lonely. She did not think her life was ruined; nevertheless, she was clueless about how to begin life anew.

For once, Bhanu cursed the solitude and isolation of Zanskar, for it denied her an escape route. She stood at some distance from the others and tried to take deep breaths to calm down, but it did not work. She looked up towards the vast sky.

The periwinkle-blue vastness from above and the whiteness from all around started to close in on her. She felt claustrophobic despite the limitless space around her. Just then, it began to snow, but her numb face could not feel the cold tinge as the snowflakes fell.

The world around her was spinning with dizzying speed. She closed her eyes to avoid the giddy feeling, but it did not help. After a few minutes, she gave up all attempts at self-control. She crashed on the hard ice with a thud and passed out.

Bhushan was the first to leap forward and reach out to Bhanu. He kneeled beside her and tried to feel her pulse through the layers of protective coverings. The others were quick to follow. As Bhushan began to slip off Bhanu's balaclava, Tsering gestured at him to step away from her. Although Tsering did not utter a word, he seemed to convey to Bhushan that Bhanu no longer felt safe in his hands.

That's what betrayal does to the traitor. It's fine as long as one gets away with deceit, but the moment it is exposed, the reprisal is punishing enough to kill one's self-esteem. The muck sticks on the traitor. A hero suddenly turns into a loathsome character.

Bhushan stepped back and watched anxiously as Tsering and the villagers attempted to revive Bhanu. The medical kit was with the trek organizers, but fortunately, aid was available in the village. The villagers—doctors without degrees, accurately diagnosed Bhanu's condition as acute mountain sickness aggravated by trauma. They administered an injection and gave her oral medicines, after which Bhanu regained consciousness; though, she wished she had not. She looked lost and haggard; her eyes were open but blank and unseeing, and she was indifferent to everything and everybody. Her reflexes were fine by then, but it seemed that she was unwilling to make use of them, lest they forced her to fully return to reality. So she lay there in total inertia, not caring much about what happened next. She avoided eye contact with anybody and refused to acknowledge Bhushan's existence.

The villagers also brought an oxygen inhaler, and after a

few minutes of catching her breath, she felt much better. The fuzziness receded quickly, lifting the fog from her mind. But that only brought back pangs of sorrow and embarrassment. She felt publicly ridiculed, humiliated.

A brief and hurried conference was held between the villagers and Tsering while the rest of the group waited anxiously on the bridge. It was decided that Bhanu would be carried to the bridge on a stretcher. The stretcher available in the village was nothing more than a worn, human-sized piece of leather with two wooden sticks inserted into loops on both sides. It was the only one the village had; nevertheless, the villagers gladly gave it to them, knowing full well that they might not get it back. They were brought up to think that whatever they possessed— whether food or a stretcher, its benefits were to be shared and that not the owner but the person who needed the resource more had the first right to it.

Four people were required to carry the stretcher. Tsering grudgingly agreed to let Bhushan handle one end, only because it meant taking the help of one less villager and thereby sparing him the trouble of the arduous two-way trek to the Nerak Bridge. Bhushan was only too willing. He knew that he had wronged her most grievously, but he would not have hesitated to give his life in order to ensure her safety and welfare. Besides, he was acutely aware that only excruciating pain would help him realize Bhanu's pain and suffering. He would have welcomed anything that inflicted severe exertion on him as punishment. What better way to begin his repentance than by carrying Bhanu across that most treacherous path?

Tsering, Bhushan and two villagers lifted Bhanu and started immediately for the bridge. Try as hard as she did, Bhanu could not avoid an occasional glance at Bhushan. She kept her eyes tightly shut—partly to avoid looking at Bhushan and partly, to stop the tears brimming in her eyes from falling. She lay on the stretcher motionless, fearing that any movement would also activate her overthinking tendencies, triggering thoughts and feelings she wanted to avoid at any cost. At the same time, she loathed her immobility because it allowed the man she hated the most, to carry her. She did not want to move her body even an inch, yet she wanted to walk independently. A slight trace of a smile crossed her face as she realized that irony.

Meanwhile, the group at the bridge was getting restive by the minute. When the trio of Bhushan, Bhanu and Tsering had not returned even after two and half hours, they were distraught. Sensing imminent trouble, one of the organizers and a trekker decided to go after them. Not discounting the chance of a mishap along the way, they mindfully carried first aid with them. They encountered the approaching party mid-way and were aghast to see Bhanu being carried on a stretcher. The organizer exclaimed, 'What the heck? What happened to Bhanu?'

Before anybody could reply, Bhanu said, 'Error of judgment. I tripped on a deceptively strong icy patch. I thought it would hold, but it proved to be unreliable. But I'm over it. I'm fine.'

Those were Bhanu's first words after regaining consciousness, but the strength and firmness in her voice surprised everyone.

The experienced organizer did not fail to notice that there was no crepe bandage around Bhanu's legs, the most elemental measure to treat a pulled muscle resulting from tripping. Obviously, Bhanu had not tripped. Tsering took the organizer and the trekker aside and explained what had happened. As he talked, he kept on giving contemptuous side-glances at Bhushan. When they returned, Bhushan had fallen in the eyes of the organizer. He was a morally upright man. His eyes conveyed contempt at Bhushan and he began to say something, but Bhanu lifted a warning hand, 'Leave it. It is—it was between him and me. In any case, it's over for good. Just take me home. I just want to be with Maa.'

Tsering and the trek organizer thanked the two villagers who had helped carry Bhanu and asked if they could retain the stretcher; Bhanu was still incapable of walking on her own. The organizer offered them money—both for their service and the stretcher, but that offended the villagers. They looked at the cash disdainfully, as if they were being paid in the wrong currency. The organizer understood. Then, using the right payment method, he warmly said 'Juleyy, Juleyy,' to the villagers and hugged them gratefully.

In Ladakh, 'Juleyy' is used to connote both 'thank you' and 'goodbye'. The villagers reciprocated with a 'Juleyy' and left for Nerak.

Nobody spoke as they hurried toward the bridge. After a while, Bhanu asked the organizer if he carried a sedative in the first aid kit. He said yes and helped Bhanu gulp a pill. Despite the load, Bhushan and the others continued to walk at a brisk pace.

The organizer had fully anticipated the horrified reaction of the group, so he took it upon himself to briefly explain to them about the developments at Nerak and Bhanu's plight thereafter. Thankfully, Bhanu was sedated, so she was beyond feeling embarrassed.

After that interaction, Bhushan's isolation from the group was total. He had become an outcast.

~

It was late afternoon. Starting the return trek then would have meant getting stranded between two overnight campsites at nightfall. So they decided to spend another night at the Nerak camp. The buffer supplies they were carrying were meant just for such unforeseen crises.

The Bhanu–Bhushan break-up had left everybody deeply disturbed; they became very withdrawn. Some effort was made to play a game or tell a story and lift the pall of gloom, but there was an absolute lack of enthusiasm. High tea passed by in a morbid atmosphere. After that, some trekkers climbed up the bridge and clicked the panoramic views with their cameras, while others just wandered around. It was essential to keep moving to keep the body warm.

Bhushan maintained his distance from the others and strolled on the riverbank aimlessly. Bhanu had come out of her slumber by then, but she pretended to be asleep when called for tea and snacks. However, the organizer forced her to get up, stretch, and walk a bit after some time. She obeyed him obligingly; she seemed the least concerned about herself.

For want of anything else to do, dinner was served early. Bhushan helped himself sparingly with food and found a rock to sit at a distance. Bhanu was made to eat unwillingly.

As soon as the sky turned dark, the group retired. Bhushan entered his tent but quickly retreated a few steps. Bhanu was not there tonight. In that split second, he realized with absolute finality that she had exited his life. Her absence hit him like a boxer's jab. He felt giddy and found a flat rock to sit on. As if to escape the flood of memories which gushed from the tent, he turned his back to it and faced the infinite darkness before him. He felt as empty as the surroundings.

In the last one week, Bhanu had become the fulcrum of his existence, but the hinges having given way, he felt his life coming apart. Unlike Bhanu, he could not handle the grief with dignity because he was guilty of wrong-doing, which Bhanu was not. And so he did what Bhanu did not do publicly—he cried. It was silent sobs initially, but as minutes passed, the sobs found a voice—a deep, wallowing, mournful sound arising from a miserable heart laden with regret, remorse and repentance.

The others who were huddled in nearby tents noticed Bhushan's solitary suffering. After a while, instead of subsiding, his despair grew frantic and louder. At the peak of anguish, Bhushan let go of all self-control and cried out, 'Maaaaaaaaaaaaaaaaaaa!'

Mother again! When faced with absolute and irretrievable loss, when there is nothing left to hold on to, the troubled child turns to Mother. And she never disappoints. Even if she is thousands of miles away, just taking her name brings immediate succour to the suffering child. Nobody in the group could sleep. They were all young hearts, susceptible to break-ups—a few had already experienced the pain. So they related with the Bhushan–Bhanu split personally. Bhushan's anguished outburst was audible, but Bhanu's agony was silent. While she showed no external signs of her plight, Richa, now back with her, could make out her face clouding a couple of times.

The temperature was dropping rapidly. Even inside the insulated tent, it was -13°C. More out of concern for Bhushan's safety than sympathy for him, one of the organizers ventured out. He coughed lightly when he reached near Bhushan and put his hand gently on his shoulders, 'Bhushan, get inside the tent.'

When Bhushan did not move, he pressed his shoulder more firmly and said, 'Bhushan get inside the tent or you will get hypothermia.'

'I want to remain out in the cold.'

'You know the effects of hypothermia?'

'Yes, but I can't face the emptiness in the tent. I would

rather remain in the cold and die.'

The organizer chided him, 'Don't be silly. Come on, get up Bhushan. Think of your father. He and your family are waiting for you.'

It was the first time anybody had thought of the other simultaneous crisis that Bhushan was facing. In the wake of the sordid break-up, Bhanu Pratap Singh's serious health condition had receded in the background. It had become secondary even for Bhushan as if his father's stroke was less critical than his break-up. But its mention suddenly made him acutely aware of the serious situation back home. He stood up in slow motion and the organizer guided him to his tent. Bhushan hesitated before getting in, like how a child fears entering a dark, cold, lifeless room. He looked at the organizer and urged him, 'I can't spend the night alone. Can you please, please be with me?'

The organizer nodded silently and gave him an encouraging squeeze on his shoulder.

In the other tent, Bhanu lay on her back in the sleeping bag and stared blankly at the hazy stars through the translucent material. Unlike four nights back, they did not seem within reach anymore, and even if they did, there was nobody she could command to pluck them for her. She shuddered a bit. It was almost imperceptible, but her watchful tentmate did detect the slight quiver followed by a muffled sob.

'You okay, Bhanu?' She asked tentatively.

Bhanu replied, 'Yes, I am fine. I don't give a fuck about him.'

There was a strange fondness even in her hateful swearing. Those who have lost out in love, especially the first love, will know that although they had walked out on an unfaithful partner, it takes a while for one to stop feeling for their ex. To let go of intense affection is a slow, painful process because the countless blissful moments of cherished togetherness and the endless caring, sharing and loving come in the way of forgetting the past. They weigh very heavily on the heart. That is why, when in love, it is better to keep your mind even as you give your heart.

~

Bhushan felt a little better in the morning. The organizer had talked to him at night and had made him promise that he would refocus on life and prioritize his family. Considering his father's condition, he was the de facto head of the family and had increased responsibilities on his shoulders. In effect, without telling it, the organizer had told Bhushan to get Bhanu out of his system, quickly. They had breakfast together. Bhanu, too, ate a little and tried to walk. After a few tentative steps, her confidence grew, and she walked more steadily.

The organizers thought it better to start the return trek even if Bhanu could not walk the whole trek; she could be carried on the stretcher whenever she felt weak or exhausted.

So, they bid adieu to Nerak and began their return trek after taking one last group picture in front of the icefall.

~

One would think that the return trek on the Chadar would be a rewind experience, like going on a long drive and coming back the same way. But Zanskar is not a concrete road; it is a living river. The surface of the Chadar is deceptively inert. There are multiple natural forces at work below and above its surface, which constantly alter its form. Certain portions of the Chadar which were smoothly traversable while the trekkers walked to Nerak, were now treacherous. At other points, flimsy ice had transformed into chunks of hard ice, safe to walk on. And at places, new mirror-clear ponds of water had formed. Although it was the same river, it had changed.

The trekkers understood this in the first couple of hours of the return trek—Zanskar did not want them to take it for granted! Hence, the spirit of adventure and challenge was retained. Rather than feeling that they were returning on the same road, the trekkers felt as if they were re-discovering the route.

It was not long before Bhanu realized that the rigour of constant walking was draining her energy very fast. At that rate, she would soon be unable to walk at all. She reasoned with the organizers that instead of walking for longer stretches, she would rather alternate between walking and being carried on the stretcher for shorter spans. That way, she would be using her energy more judiciously. The trekkers agreed and formed two teams of four members each who would carry Bhanu in turns. The ninth member, Bhushan, was left out. He looked hurt, but the organizer who had remained with him during the night put his hand around his shoulders and said softly, 'It is all right mate, let it pass.'

'I don't deserve this!' Bhushan remarked bitterly.

The organizer said, 'I understand, but you can't escape people's judgment for what you have done to Bhanu. It is natural for them to side with her. You don't have a choice Bhushan, you will have to accept rejection. Get Bhanu out of your system, the sooner the better for you.'

After a pause, he reminded him, 'You have the other crisis to deal with, so focus on your family now.'

Bhushan said wryly, 'Reality check—thanks. So where does one go from here?'

The organizer continued, 'Refocus. Realign your priorities.

Pay attention to your family and your dad. They need you; Bhanu does not need you anymore. Go where you are needed, Bhushan and stay there. If you chase people who don't want you and go after situations that don't require you, you are going to be rejected. Without knowing your reasons for what you did to her and why you did it, I would say move on in life. In the next few days we will be back in Delhi. While parting, we will hug each other warmly and slap backs spiritedly and say good bye, not knowing whether we will ever meet again or remain in touch. That is why I don't want to pass a judgment on whatever happened. But take it from me as a well-wisher; life is much more than a broken affair. Years from now, you will realize in hindsight that heartbreaks are valuable life mentors; pain is inevitable to any process of growth and evolution. So grow up and evolve.'

Bhushan remained silent, lost deep in thought. He was readying for a life without Bhanu and Bunty and Babli. After a while, he took a deep breath and said to the organizer, 'Thank you.'

The gentleman replied light-heartedly, 'That will be 500, in dollars.'

Bhushan smiled after what seemed like ages.

Lunch and high tea came and went. Everybody had become reticent, focused on keeping to the trek schedule. The group's jovial temperament had mellowed, replaced by a cultivated calm. The common concern of the group now was to reach Chilling and then Leh as soon as possible.

Night came, and with it came darkness in Bhushan's and Bhanu's hearts. While the day had passed in routine activities that distracted their minds, the solitary suffering returned with the night. It was as if memories had conspired to attack both Bhanu and Bhushan simultaneously.

Bhushan realized that his daytime succour infused by the organizer was temporary; it could not hold up against the sharp pangs of Bhanu's thoughts. A couple of times, he did succeed in shunning Bhanu from his thoughts, but she returned with a vengeance after a while, and when that happened, the pain was worse than before. Bhushan thought that any effort to forget her was like a painkiller—when its effect had worn off, the pain resurfaced in bouts. He thought that rather than forcing her out of his thoughts, it would better to let them be. Then the pain would be evenly spread and hence less unbearable.

Bhanu too was left bleeding by the barrage of thoughts about Bhushan.

Her courage during the day seemed pretentious at night. She was alone now and unseen by others, so she could drop the mask. No sooner than he came in her thoughts, she felt hollow from within and a sinking feeling overtook her. The pull of despair was very forceful but she tried hard to remain afloat. The effort cost her all the energy that remained in her after the day's rigours. Past midnight, she lay in her sleeping bag like a sack, overcome by mental and physical exhaustion. A couple of times, she hallucinated that he was actually there, his handsome face within her arm's reach—she actually tried to brush his hair lightly, his throaty laughter ringing in her ears, his scent palpable in the enclosed air of the tent. Then, she blinked forcefully a few times to wish him away. However, he kept returning. Ultimately, like Bhushan, she gave up trying, and when she let her mind access his memories at will, her suffering eased, much like the pain that levelled out in Bhushan's heart.

It was then that Bhanu resentfully conceded to herself—she missed Bhushan sorely. Her tough exterior was a make-believe act for others' benefit. The thought made her hate herself as much as she hated him. She shuddered. Like the previous night, the slight quiver was noticed by her tent-mate who lay awake behind closed eyes. She let a few seconds pass, then turned to Bhanu and asked with concern, 'You okay, Bhanu?'

And just like the previous night, Bhanu replied, 'Yes, no worries. I don't give a damn about that jerk.'

Bhanu had summoned adequate resolve and loathing in her tone to sound convincing. She had decided that that would be her default reply throughout the rest of the trek to whoever inquired whether she was fine. And she would maintain her cool from outside. How she felt from inside was her business, not theirs. Her grief was very private, and she intended to keep it that way. She was sure to get over it slowly once she was home.

The next morning, the group readied for the trek by nine. Bhanu had lain awake the whole night and did not feel like walking, so she requested the stretcher. Just as it was being unfolded and laid out, Bhushan, who was standing at a distance, stepped forward to volunteer to carry Bhanu. She immediately shot a spiteful look at him which froze him. Her eyes narrowed, creases appeared on her forehead as she frowned hatefully and muttered under her breath, words hissing out of narrow spaces between her clenched teeth, 'Don't you dare!'

He took a step back. Tsering then took his place and the group started their trek.

By then, Bhushan had come to terms with his rejection. Even the organizer, the only one to talk to him, had made it clear that he was in no way siding with him. He was merely helping him see through the maze—presenting an objective picture of the situation and offering some advice as a well-wisher. Even then, it helped Bhushan a lot in grasping and coming to terms with the reality. He began to accept that he was the sole perpetrator of the mess that was created in Bhanu's and his life. In a candid moment, he even accepted that he would have looked down upon a betrayer just as he was being denounced by others.

The more Bhushan delved into his break-up, the more painful it became, until he could not bear it anymore. It was then that he decided to heed the organizer's advice. There is no undo button, he told himself, let me try the forward tab.

The path ahead led to his family. His father, Bhanu Pratap Singh lay in the ICU like a vegetable; he would probably never regain consciousness. And his only child was not even thinking about him!

'When would you think of your father, when it is too late?' he rebuked himself.

As his heart reached out to his beloved father, a flood of childhood memories gushed into his mind, as he remembered his father's sacrifices to give him a good life.

Bhanu Pratap Singh was a self-made man who had started from the base of the ladder. In his early days as a textile trader, he had been cheated badly and banished from a partnership. The misfortune had ruined him. He had become an emotional and financial wreck. His mother had then taken the reins of the household in her hands. She worked as a home tutor which fetched ₹430 a month, just enough to keep their heads above the water. Cooking was limited to once a day. Buying class IV textbooks for Bhushan was unthinkable; he studied from books borrowed for a night from his classmates.

Bhushan remembered a particular birthday when his mother had not been able to buy some toffees for him to distribute amongst his classmates. During recess, some abusive classmates had called him, 'Bhushan the beggar'.

'Even beggars are better off than him,' another one had chided.

The leader among them, to prove that he was better than the rest, had sneeringly retorted, 'Ask your father to beg at the railway station, and let him take your mother with him.'

Nobody can listen to their mother's name being slandered. Bhushan recalled how, at the bully's taunt he had lost his self-control. Something primal had snapped inside him. He had lunged at the leader of the gang in white rage, pinned him down and started punching him. The other had two tried to stop him but in that moment his outrage overpowered reason. It was only when Bhushan saw the blood streaming from the other boy's nose had he suddenly realized that he had gone too far. By then, the principal had reached the scene. He had ordered Bhushan to his office. Bhushan had remained uncommunicative during the questioning, so his parents had been called. By the time Bhanu Pratap Singh and his wife had reached the school, Bhushan's rustication letter was ready. After endless pleas on their part, the principal had reduced Bhushan's punishment to a an unconditional written apology, a promise from his parents that Bhushan would never behave in that manner again and a fine of ₹500.

₹500! When the parents had begged the principal to lower the amount, he had said, 'You can either pay the fine or you can take your son and walk out of here.'

Bhanu Pratap's frantic pleas for help had gone unheard or unanswered by friends and family. It is true that they all offer an umbrella only after it has stopped raining. In the end, Bhanu Pratap had had no option but to sell his wife's silver ornaments, which included a beautifully engraved heirloom bracelet that was gifted by her grandmother at the time of their wedding. Bhushan recalled that night's conversation between his parents that he had overheard from the living room. His father had told his mother in choked voice, 'These are the best years of your life, but look at me, instead of buying you something valuable, I am forcing you to part with your last pieces of jewellery.'

Bhushan had heard his father's muffled sobs and had pressed his ears to their bedroom wall. His mother had comforted his father, 'Don't say that, my darling. Wouldn't you have done the same in my place? Bhushan is our only child. These ornaments are just metal. I would give my life to save him from trouble.'

Sometimes, words of comfort work the other way round. Rather than soothing a person, they drag them deeper in self-pity. Bhanu Pratap had lamented, 'We are living off your income and that weight is crushing me. Now I have made you sell your ornaments. I would rather prefer to…'

Bhushan, even as a child had sensed that his mother had put her hand over his father's mouth to prevent dark words from coming out, 'Sssshhh, Don't, *don't*,' she had said, 'When we got married, we had promised to stand by each other, come what may. This metal has no value for me if it can't help us save our child.'

The air in their room had been thick with sorrow. His mother had tried to lighten the moment, 'Now stop blaming yourself. Our life will change for the better soon. And then, don't think I am going to let you off cheaply. In place of these ten silver ornaments and our ancestral bracelet, I am going to demand ten kilos of gold. Not a bad bargain! Now give me that crooked, dimpled smile of yours.'

As if the heavens were eavesdropping on their conversation and had decided to favour the couple, Bhanu Pratap's luck changed for the better after that night. He bounced back very fast. In just two years, he was out of debt, and soon thereafter, the family had moved to a respectable address in Kalkaji. Bhushan's mother had had all the gold she wanted, but more than that, she had her man with a golden heart.

Even as the family got better off with each passing year, that night's conversation between his parents had stayed in Bhushan's mind and grew on him with time. It was a defining incident that had made him proud of his parents. He had vowed to himself that night that he would never do anything that would embarrass his parents.

And today… he thought, not only had he hurt Bhanu but also diminished his family's honour.

In the other tent, Bhanu, too, was lost in childhood memories. Like Bhushan, she had had a modest upbringing. Her family had had its own share of struggle and at times, making both ends meet had been a problem. Because of their educational qualifications, her parents had stuck to their academic careers. Teaching in a school or college was not a materially lucrative occupation in those days. On top of it, they had the burden of maintaining Dr Bhutia's extended family. His blind father, an aged widower, also lived with them.

The family's difficulties had suddenly multiplied when Dr Bhutia was falsely implicated in some financial irregularity in the college and was suspended, pending departmental inquiry. He was entitled to only half of his paltry salary during the suspension period.

Bhanu remembered her grandfather's birthday, when her mother could barely manage to prepare a sweet dish of a couple of ripe bananas sautéed in ghee with a sprinkling of ground sugar. When prepared, the quantity had been reduced to a little over a few tablespoonfuls. As had been the custom in those days, her mother had to served her father-in-law's plate first and had asked Bhanu to take it to him. Most of the sweet dish was already served in that plate and there was hardly anything left for the others. Bhanu recalled how she was so overcome by the sweet aroma of her favourite dish that she had gulped down the entire quantity in a few hasty mouthfuls before handing the dish to Dadaji. Her child's mind had thought that since there were no remains of the sweet dish in the plate, Dadaji would never come to know that the item was there at all! But the elderly sightless man had had the habit of feeling the contents of his plate before starting to eat. When his hands touched the greasy surface where the sweetened bananas had been served, he immediately knew their fate! Observing his expressions, Bhanu knew that he knew. She had mumbled feebly, 'Sorry Dadaji'

It is said that the interest on the capital is always dearer than the capital itself. Bhanu was very dear to her Dadaji, he had always doted over her and often used to shared his meals with her. Upon hearing Bhanu's meek apology, his unseeing eyes had welled up and he had hugged Bhanu tightly, and said in his native Lepcha dialect something like, 'You, who have eaten the sweet dish, may the Almighty transfer all the sweetness from my remaining life to yours.'

Mother had heard this and rushed out of the kitchen. She was in no position to prepare the dish again; there was no ghee or bananas in the kitchen. Utter helplessness and frustration had overtaken her normally calm demeanour and she had slapped Bhanu, the first and the last time she ever did that. Dadaji had quickly intervened, siding with Bhanu, 'Oh, don't be so harsh on the child. She is at no fault.'

Bhanu's mother had replied, 'Pitaji, please don't take sides. She has ruined your birthday.'

The usually calm and composed elderly man had replied in a slightly raised voice, 'You call this ruining my day? On the contrary she has made my day. As it is, I have no desire left to appease my taste buds, and my heart would have been torn if I ate it all and my angel child was left deprived. Don't create any issue and please don't say anything about this to my son. The sweet dish has gone to the one who deserved it.'

After that, he quickly regained his composure and ate the rest of his meal silently with contentment. When he had finished, he called Bhanu to sit beside him and had told her a fairytale about a winged fairy who prepared a lovely birthday card for her grandfather and placed it beneath his pillow the night before the birthday. Early morning the next day, the grandfather habitually woke up the fairy to take her out for a walk. When they reached an opening in the woods, they saw a cane basket wrapped in silk placed beside a tree trunk. The fairy was amused and puzzled to see the basket, so the grandfather asked her to untie the cloth. As soon as she did that, many beautiful butterflies flocked out of it. For a few moments, there was a riot of colours all around them. The grandfather bent and whispered in the fairy's ears, 'My angel this is my return gift to you. Thank you for the lovely card.'

The overjoyed fairy covered her grandpa in a bear hug.

Bit by bit, watered by such incidents, Bhanu's upbringing had been nurtured with the virtue of respectful living within one's means. Bhanu's pride for her parents had not waned while growing up in a metro city amidst so many external influences. On the contrary, as she grew up, she had become more aware of her family's values which had made her what she was—a self-assured young lady with a keen sense of righteousness.

That night in Zanskar, the incident replayed in Bhanu's mind as if it had occurred recently. Although her Dadaji was long gone, she could feel him beside her. That illusion calmed her immediately. She looked up at the stars from the tent's translucent material and mouthed, 'Dadaji I miss you'

~

Around lunch, the group encountered the Zanskari ladies who were returning after leaving their children at the boarding school in Leh. At first, there was just a hint of their rhythmic, melodious singing in the air, but as they came near, the melody became clearer. Although it was a different song, its oneness with the surroundings was just the same. No sooner did the ladies see the trekkers, than they waved at them cheerfully. When within earshot, loud, hearty Juleyys were exchanged, as if long-lost friends were reuniting. Bhanu's mood lifted on seeing them. The young mother asked her, 'How are you, madam?'

Bhanu replied with the help of Tsering, 'I am very good and how are you all?'

'We are also very fine. Nature has been kind to us.'

Then Bhanu inquired about the infant, 'How is the baby?'

'She is fine now. She had caught a cold but after giving the medicine at Leh, she is all right now.'

Bhanu adored baby girls. She asked if she could hold her for a while and the mother unhesitatingly said yes. Bhanu cradled it close to her bosom and patted her lovingly, humming a lullaby in her lovely voice. The infant responded instantly and gave Bhanu a toothless smile. She smiled back and pinched her rosy cheeks, asking the mother, 'What is her name?'

'Tashi,' the mother replied in a proud voice, making it sound very important.

'Oh such a sweet name and what does it mean?'

Tsering said, 'It means "young lady", memshaab.'

'How appropriate!' Then, turning to the mother, Bhanu asked, 'And what is your name?'

'Jigmet.'

'Lovely name. How old is Tashi, Jigmet?'

'Around eight months.'

'I thought she is over a year! You have been blessed with a beautiful, healthy angel. And where is her Papa?'

'He is a climber. He has gone with a mountaineers' group to earn. It's been months now.'

Bhanu asked, 'So Jigmet, how do you handle life with your husband gone away for so long? It is almost like being a single mother.'

Jigmet replied, 'We mountain people have learned to live with less of everything, including love. But then, what is less and what is more in love? I love my man completely, so I can love him even if I am a hundred mountains away from him. I can be with him any moment that I wish. Love is not love if it lets peaks and valleys separate two hearts. That is our simple understanding of love—it can rise above boundaries and borders. And besides, Bhanu madam, the village lives as a family. When someone is in trouble, the entire village becomes one to get that person out of trouble. We may own nothing in your comparison, but we have been happily settled in our world since centuries. So what if my man is absent, the whole village and the reverent Goba'—Tsering said it meant the village head—'are my protectors. Above all, the mountains and the spirits of our ancestors don't let any harm descend on us.'

Bhanu was overwhelmed by the wisdom of this native woman. She marvelled that in this remote, ancient world, everything was for keeps, especially love.

Jigmet then noticed that Bhanu and Bhushan were not together as before, and asked innocently why it was so. Bhanu simply replied that they had decided to remain separate. However, the implication was lost on Jigmet's naïve mind. It was incomprehensible for her that two persons could fall in and out of love within days. For her, love was a lifelong bond. So she asked again, why they were not sitting together like last time. Then Bhanu told her that something terrible had happened between them and they had decided to end their love.

'Bhanu Madam, Love is not water stored in a pot which can be turned on or off with a tap. Love is like water in a river, which flows continuously. The river cannot rest even for a moment; neither can it go back in its journey. It has to go on and on continuously, that is its nature. That is the nature of true love.

She paused for a moment, then took Bhanu's hand in hers and said, 'Tell me what happened, nomo-le.'

Jigmet had no idea that such direct questions were considered uncivilized in the world beyond the mountains. Knowing that, Bhanu did not mind Jigmet's directness at all; she knew it was straight from the heart, a genuine concern. She was also moved by Jigmet's 'nomo-le' address for her, which meant younger sister. However, the pain was too fresh to let her narrate the incident in first person. She looked at Tsering, asking for help, and he took Jigmet aside to talk to her for a few minutes.

When they returned, tears were rolling down Jigmet's cheeks. Mountain people cry easily. She patted Bhanu's back affectionately, like a real older sister, and said, 'Tserka macho,' which means, 'don't be sad'.

Bhanu nodded silently, biting her lower lip, fighting tears. Jigmet took Bhanu to a stone seat and made her sit there. Then she said something which Bhanu would never forget, 'Madam, we are not forward-minded and modern like you. We have lived here in Zanskar for centuries without knowing what progress the outside world has made. I will live my insignificant life and die one day without making a difference to anybody or anything. We are among the most ordinary and unintelligent backward people on this earth. We live life in a simple and uncomplicated way and keep a distance from anything that is beyond our understanding. So as per my simple thinking, love is forever. Once in love, always in love, and I add, with the same person. Look all around Zanskar, Madam, and you will know what I mean. The mighty mountains and the snow clinging to it have loved each other timelessly, the clouds and the sky are inseparable, air and its coldness cannot be taken apart ever. We have learned how to love from the elements around us. They have taught us that there can be no second love, we love only once, and that first love is so strong that not even the cruellest of storms can separate the snow from the mountains or the cold from the air.'

Jigmet was a natural storyteller. She was so engrossed in her talk that she failed to notice that Bhanu's eyes were wet. When she looked at Bhanu, she realized that her words had scratched Bhanu's fresh wound. Gently, she wiped off Bhanu's tears and said, 'Sorry for hurting you.'

Bhanu gave her a weak smile, 'Never mind sister, I am all right now. Thank you for your affection.'

Suddenly, it occurred to Bhanu to offer lunch to the ladies. She had a quick word with the organizers and invited them to share noodles and tea. It was a feast for Jigmet and her companions. They ate without inhibition, as they did everything else in life. Bhanu wondered when they would have had their last proper meal. After three servings, she offered them more noodles but they refused, not out of courtesy but because they could not eat any more. Bhanu asked Jigmet if she had a container, and she produced a large plastic cup from her tattered sling bag. Bhanu filled it with noodles and gave it back, saying playfully, 'One for the road!'

Finally, the ladies were ready to depart. Both the groups exchanged hearty Juleyys. Just then, one of the organizers thought of returning the stretcher to Nerak if Bhanu did not need it any more. She said she was feeling fine, so the ladies took back the stretcher. They quickly loaded it with their backpacks.

A thought crossed Bhanu's mind, these people travelled so light through life that all their belongings could fit into a stretch of worn leather!

The four ladies took charge of the four sides of the stretcher, while Tashi sat pretty on it. When they were almost about to disappear into the mountains, they put the stretcher down, turned back and waved at the trekkers for the last time. Jigmet shouted at Bhanu, 'Madam, may the holy spirits of Zanskar bestow comfort and peace on your hurt heart.'

And the mountains echoed her affection.

~

When the trekkers reached Tilad Do, two SUVs were ready to take them to Leh. They were divided into two groups and started settling down in the vehicles. It was the first time in a fortnight that they would not be traveling on feet!

In Leh, they spent a day lazing around. Tsering departed for his village in the afternoon. When he approached Bhanu, he could only say, 'Take care, memshaab.'

Instead of replying, Bhanu took him in a bear hug and said, 'I will, and you also take care. Now go, before I start crying.'

At dinner, Bhushan followed Bhanu—he badly wanted to meet her once before they parted. When she was within earshot, he told her, 'I want to talk to you one last time.'

Bhanu had a to make a supreme effort not to let her feelings show on her face. She did not acknowledge his presence and quickly walked away.

Bhushan turned to the table where the organizer was seated and said, 'May I?'

The organizer smiled and gestured at him to sit, then opened the conversation, 'So how is it going Bhushan?'

Bhushan came straight to the point, 'Sir I need your help. As you can understand, it is very important for me to talk to Bhanu once. I don't expect dramatic turnarounds from the talk and that is not my purpose any way. My only intention is to clear certain things with her. I may not get another chance. If I don't talk to her now it will bother me all my life that the only girl I loved truly, hates me all her life. Sir, please, I need your help to arrange a brief talk with Bhanu.'

The organizer replied thoughtfully, 'Okay, I don't mind having a word with her but I cannot guarantee results.'

'I don't have anything more to lose, Sir' Bhushan replied matter-of-factly.

The organizer knew that persuading Bhanu to meet Bhushan would be very difficult if not impossible. He had never thought that his mountaineering career would also include playing the role of a peacemaker! But he resolved to give it his best try.

The group was to leave for Delhi the next day around noon. A brunch of jalebis, chhole-puri, pulao and curry was arranged the next day, after which the trekkers could indulge in shopping. The organizer walked up to where Bhanu was sitting and bowed theatrically, 'Bhanu! May I?'

She smiled at his charm and said, 'Sir, please.'

'Congratulations!' the organizer said as he sat down, 'You have completed a very difficult track, now what about life's marathon?'

Bhanu could immediately get a whiff of where this was leading. Her voice lost its warmth, 'Sir, has Bhushan sent you?'

Then she realized that her reaction was impulsive, 'Sorry Sir, I did not mean to be harsh, but I will not be comfortable talking if this is initiated by him.'

The organizer covered it up, 'No Bhanu, I came to you on my own. I just meant to ask you, what next in life?'

Bhanu relaxed, 'Sir, I am trying to focus on my master's degree and my career now.'

The organizer, 'That's how it should be, but Bhanu, I am asking about life, and life is more than a career.'

Bhanu spoke more mindfully, 'Sir, to be honest, I am emotionally stunted at the moment. I am surviving on a daily basis. I can hardly look beyond my nose, so to say. I am not willing to go through the effort of taking a long-term view of life; it is too taxing. But I do know this much, my career will be my life henceforth. Whatever happened is behind me. I have already punched the undo button.'

The organizer pondered, 'I will tell you what I told Bhushan some days back—I am nobody to judge; I don't want to delve into what is fair and unfair. I have only your welfare at heart. Such incidents do leave behind scars. It varies from person to person how deep they are and how soon they heal. I have a feeling that you will heal very quickly. You are a courageous young lady full of confidence, determination and grit. This is not hollow praise, Bhanu. However, having said that, one can't expect everybody to be as strong as you. Two persons have suffered in this break-up…'

'Only one of them deserved to suffer.'

He conceded, 'Yes it is true that there is usually no break-up without an innocent and a guilty party. But the innocent emerges stronger than the guilty by the sheer strength of innocence. Besides, the guilt makes it more difficult for the guilty to overcome the emotional crisis.'

Bhanu shrugged, 'That's the problem of the guilty.'

'I agree. But Bhanu, it is not about letting him get away, it is about helping him get over…'

'Help???' Bhanu could not help sounding exasperated. Had it been anyone else than the organizer, she would have thought he was abetting Bhushan's betrayal.

He let it pass and continued, 'When a criminal accepts not only the verdict but also his crime, it shows he is in repentance. If he wishes to meet the victim to express his repentance, the onus falls on the victim to be high-minded and grant him the meeting. It gives the criminal the chance to cleanse his conscience and perhaps explain why he did what he did.

'I don't mean to imply that what Bhushan did was justified and that you should accept and forgive him the way he is. But in the very least, try to understand why he did what he did.'

He paused to let it sink into Bhanu's mind, and then resumed, 'It is only a hearing that he is asking for Bhanu. Believe me, he is acutely aware of his wrongdoing and perhaps he himself thinks it's not worthy of pardon, much less, reconciliation. I urge you, please think about it before we all part. Who knows? It might even help you move on with lesser hatred and a lighter heart—you know, letting go of loss with a large and forgiving heart.'

Bhanu was listening with rapt attention now.

He then wrapped it up with something profound, 'Bhanu, let us not forget that we are all humans, we are not above erring. In some way or the other, at some point in our lives, we will wrong others. Try to imagine your plight if the person whom you have wronged doesn't heed your request to be heard. Think about it before you take your final decision.'

That softened Bhanu's stand. However, she was not ready for the meeting, 'Maybe you are right, sir. But as I said earlier, I can't think straight right now. I am bound to be negatively biased toward him and you can't blame me for that. But even if I agree with you, I cannot bring myself to meet him, at least not so soon. I don't have the capacity for a face-off with him. Of course I loathe him, but I fear I still love him involuntarily—it was my first love after all. If I meet him, I may go to either of the extremes, I may slap him hard or I may rush into his arms, and I want to avoid doing both, I simply don't have enough of emotional energy in me right now. It's my worst fear Sir, I don't want to start loving him again.'

Her voice trailed off. When she picked it up again, her words were halting, 'No, sir—I cannot, I don't want to—it's too scary. Let it be this way—please.'

He offered Bhanu water, and resumed after she took a few sips, 'Your honesty is very touching, Bhanu. I don't know whether I deserve your trust or not, thank you. I understand your situation.'

He remained deep in thought, and Bhanu remained silent. After a while, his face brightened a bit and he said, 'I have a suggestion, Bhanu, a middle way out.'

Bhanu was resigned and weary, 'No sir, please don't push me into this, I am already feeling weak-kneed.'

'Look Bhanu, I am not saying you agree with my suggestion, but please at least hear me out.'

Bhanu shrugged nonchalantly.

'If it is not a problem, I will remain present during the meeting. That way, the talk will refrain from getting too personal and getting out of hand.'

She thought over it, then said, 'Sir, can this not be avoided?'

'Believe me Bhanu, from Bhushan's point of view, this is absolutely necessary. Let's not forget that he is also facing another equally grave crisis at the moment, his father is on his deathbed. He is literally torn apart by the twin tragedies. And even you will agree that after this, he may not get a second chance to talk to you. You will be very noble by agreeing to meet him.'

Bhanu kept staring at the glass of water for long, her face sombre, her gaze fixed, as if waiting for a message to emerge from within her. She was fighting an intense inner battle. When it ended, she raised her face, looked into the organizer's eyes and said, 'Okay. Okay sir, I don't mind.'

'Phew,' The organizer let out a huge sigh of relief.

~

The rendezvous was arranged at one of south Delhi's many coffee shops. It was evening, and the shadows had started lengthening. Bhushan was already there, seated in the farthest corner, nervousness written all over his face. The partially open sunblind was casting an angled, graphic play of light and shade on his table. Bhanu trailed behind the organizer and was literally in his shadow as they approached Bhushan. He got up, nodded awkwardly at them and muttered, 'Thank you for coming.'

The organizer greeted him and gestured Bhanu to slide inside while he sat opposite Bhushan.

Bhushan's eyes were fixed on Bhanu. He was staring at her and it made her extremely uncomfortable. His opening line to her was a blunder; he addressed her by the nickname he had given her, 'Bhalu, how are you?'

Bhanu glared at him, her eyes like red-hot embers. It was a near-fatal faux pas.

Sensing imminent disaster, the organizer passed a strict cautionary glance at Bhushan, while patting Bhanu's shoulder reassuringly, as if to say this won't happen again.

Bhanu spoke without looking at Bhushan, 'Let's do away with clumsy pleasantries. Come to the point.'

The attendant came to take the order. Bhushan and the organizer opted for hot coffee with chocolate sauce. Bhanu said she didn't want anything, but when the organizer whispered, 'It's on me', she ordered mint tea.

The moment he left, the organizer set the tone of the conversation, 'Bhushan wants to apologise for whatever happened in Zanskar, and also wants to say something about the reasons behind his wrongdoing.'

Bhushan began, 'Bhanu, I never wanted anything as badly as to express my sincerest apologies for what happened in Zanskar. I am repenting it with all my heart. It is up to you whether you believe in my sincerity or not, and whether you accept my apology or not, but the mere fact that I got this chance to tell you how sorry I am, is a big relief for me.'

She remained impassive. He took a breather and continued, 'Thank you for coming. It has lifted a very heavy burden from my heart. I will be able to breathe easily for the rest of my life.'

Bhanu was finding his words practised, perhaps even insincere. She interrupted, 'And the burden on my heart is heavier for the same reason, for coming here and giving you this chance. Gosh, I feel guilty of being too lenient with myself but anyway that's my problem, I have promised Sir that I will sit it out, so go on, but make it brief.'

'I reckon that. I reckon that my mistake...'

Bhanu's eyes narrowed and her forehead creased, 'Mistake, eh? Is that all you made? As in, you forgot to take the right turn and lost your way, is it? Actually, it is my mistake that I let you take me for a ride. But any way accept that it was a well-thought strategy to keep me in the dark, not a mistake. Everybody makes mistakes and they are forgivable, but not everybody indulges in premeditated duplicity, and that is not pardonable.'

'I'm sorry,' Bhushan mumbled.

Bhanu was clearly edgy, 'Oh stop using that word in your every line.' Then, looking at the organizer, she said, 'Sir, please tell him to finish fast, you know my reasons for not being able to take this for too long. Ask him if he has anything more to say than sorry.'

The waiter brought orders.

Bhushan tried to be more sorted, 'Bhanu, I did not tell you about Brinda because I felt you will never accept my love if you knew about her, and I just could not bring myself to accept a no as an answer from you. However, it was not that I wanted to keep you in the dark. I was waiting for a more appropriate time to tell you about her.'

'Appropriate time, more appropriate time!' Bhanu felt like screaming, 'So when would've been an appropriate time to reveal your mystery woman to me? After having slept with me and promising me the moon and making me dream about your children? When you would have taken total control of my emotions so that I would become gullible and dependent on you, is that when you would have told me about her? So that it would be easier for you to exploit the situation, with me on my knees, begging you not to desert me, and you not relenting until I was ready to play second fiddle to your Brinda?'

Bhushan sought to correct her 'No, no, Bhanu I honestly wanted to tell you as soon as possible, it was just a matter of time…'

Controlling herself with great effort, Bhanu repeated after him, 'It was just a matter of time, huh?'

Her hands were a bit shaky as she lifted her drink to take a sip.

Bhushan continued, 'Yes, believe me, I loved you too much to lose you. You were all that I had ever dreamed in my love. My betrothal with Brinda was an arrangement of mutual convenience between two known families. It had nothing to do with my personal liking.'

'Then why did you accept the alliance?'

'I was cajoled and pushed into accepting it.'

'Prime time soap material.'

'Yes, one could say that.'

Then Bhanu changed tracks, 'Well, I am just wondering, what if I would have played along and continued with the relationship even after you had told me about Brinda, how would you have dealt with her in telling her about me?'

Bhushan replied, 'I had already decided how to do it. I would have first spoken with my parents and shown them how mismatched Brinda and I were. How she and I did not share anything in common, that she suited the family, not me. Then I would have talked to Brinda and told her that our marriage had no future. I would have opted out of it Bhanu, even if I had never fallen in love with you. I would have convinced Brinda that the alliance was grossly unfair to her because she would never get a loving husband out of it. The sooner the sham was put to an end, the better it would be for everyone.'

'Look who is talking about being fair! About not cheating women! Do you even realize that you have already cheated two women? That's some fairness, ha! And what if either your parents or Brinda or both of them would have refused to buy your logic? Where would I have been in your scheme of things then?'

That was typically Bhanu, sharp and pointed. Bhushan was not expecting it and was caught off-guard. He took a moment to reply and then fumbled, 'Well in that case…'

'Well, in that case what?'

'In that case, I…'

Bhanu edged forward in her chair and leaned toward Bhushan, her eyes liquid red, 'Yes, in that case?'

Bhushan was shaken by Bhanu's aggressiveness. His mind fogged and went blank. He remained tongue-tied for a few seconds, and Bhanu mistook it as his guilt. She prodded him in a hoarse voice cracking with rage and hatred, 'Yes?'

Completely disoriented by then, not knowing what he was saying, Bhushan said, 'Well, in that case, family first.'

Those words were too cruel on Bhanu. She almost slapped herself for wanting to rush into Bhushan's arms when they entered the café. Her hatred of him was complete. She let out a low, scornful self-directed laugh and said, 'So I was your plan B after all.'

Then she got up and walked out of Bhushan's life for the second time.

5

Mother's Love Helps To Get Over Other Love

Unlike Zanskar, here, Bhanu had the option of running away from the scene. She went straight to the boarding house, packed up and headed for the airport. She had managed a window seat on one of the late-evening flights to Mumbai. She bought herself something to drink, settled in the waiting area and then called home. She heard the voice she wanted to hear the most and went limp with relief, 'Mom.'

Her mother sprang up in delight on hearing Bhanu's voice and launched a breathless monologue, 'Oh Bhanu darling, how lovely to hear your voice! How are you and where are you? How was Zanskar? I guess you are supposed to be in Delhi today and tomorrow for shopping and all, so shop until you drop darling. If possible peep into some new shops in Hauz Khas, they have some very trendy stuff you will love. And then come home soon, my arms are eager to embrace you my child. It seems like ages…'

Bhanu interrupted her mother, 'No Mom, I am not going shopping, I am returning home today. In fact I am at the airport waiting for my flight. Pick me up at the airport 10-ish.'

Mother was immediately concerned, 'What happened, Bhanu? I am worried.'

'Nothing mom, seriously, it's just that I'm missing you sorely.'

But her mother knew better. Mothers always know better. Aloud, she just said, 'Okay I will be at the airport. I too miss you sorely darling. Bye then, hug you soon.'

~

The flight was uneventful, the glossy airline magazine boring, the food bland and stale, the smiles of hostesses plastic, and the low-pitched, constant in-flight humming annoying. After about fifty minutes, the airplane hit an air pocket. Bhanu welcomed the change—at least it produced some sense of life in the static mid-air environment. She looked out of the window. The darkness was impregnable; she could actually feel it transforming the sky into a black sea of nothingness. As it is, air travel was not Bhanu's first choice—it was too predictable and monotonous, there was nothing at all to look forward to from the window, and it always left her head numb. Speed was the only thing going in favour of air travel, and speed was what Bhanu needed the most at that time. She had shut herself from every other thought and emotion except the anticipation of being with her mother.

When the aircraft touched the ground, Bhanu tried to imagine what her mother would be wearing—perhaps a pastel coloured churidar suit. When she spotted her, she was indeed wearing a plain crème suit. They rushed into each other's arms. This was the moment Bhanu had been longing for since that day in Nerak. She felt like a cub nestling under mother lioness's belly in the shade of a giant tree on a hot summer day. Her mother's warmth acted like a balm on her aching heart, but it also melted emotions which Bhanu had managed to freeze until then. One look at Bhanu's face after they broke the hug, and mother could make out that her child had been through hell. However, she decided not to press Bhanu for details immediately. Instead, she said, 'Welcome home darling, how was your adventure? You look so tanned and famished, didn't they feed you properly?'

Bhanu said, 'I am glad I'm home mom, truly, and Zanskar was divine and they did feed us well. But I know what you mean. I needed to lose a little weight anyway, so here I am, as fit as a fiddle.'

As soon as they were in the car, Bhanu let go of her restrain and broke down. Before her mother could start the ignition, Bhanu grabbed her arm, buried her face in her bosom, and let out her anguish. Her kohl got smeared, staining her mother's new dress, but it did not matter. Her mother held her tightly, protectively, caressing her hair and forehead and wiping her tears all at once, muttering tender, soothing words like, 'My child.'

Or simply, 'It's all right, it's all right.'

When Bhanu was better, her mother gently pulled her apart and said, 'It's all right darling, people are getting curious around us; shall I drive now?'

Bhanu noticed the glances of passers-by with embarrassment, wiped her tears and straightened in her seat. Mother then started the car.

Dr Bhutia was away on a lecture tour, so when they reached home, Bhanu and her mother took the luggage in. Then Bhanu went straight to her favourite armchair in the veranda and plonked herself in it. She felt a lot better in the comfort of her home.

She closed her eyes, lay inert in the armchair, blanked out her mind, and let the homely feeling wash over her. The creepers and the plants and the three wind chimes made the therapy more effective.

Mother called out from the kitchen, 'Dinner is ready.'

Bhanu replied without opening her eyes that she had had some food in the flight and wanted just coffee.

Mother came with coffee after a while. She was too worried to postpone their conversation, 'Okay Bhanu, will you be comfortable telling me what's bothering you?'

Bhanu opened her eyes, came out of her cocoon, and came right to the point, 'Mum, in short, I met a guy during the trek, fell in love and got cheated on.'

'That's really short, but anyway, it all happened in fifteen days?' Her mother had an expression of disbelief on her face.

'Actually, less than that.'

'You take more time than that to decide on a new handset.'

Bhanu did not respond, so mother prodded her again, 'Okay, so who was he?'

'Bhushan Bhanu Pratap Singh.'

She was surprised at how easily her mind could stray into the forbidden land of cherished memories. There were miles to go before she could look back at her past dispassionately, without being pained by it. Until then, she had to keep her mind under a tight leash.

Her mother repeated, 'Hmmmm, Bhushan Bhanu Pratap Singh.'

And Bhanu knew she would Google out his name later. She continued, 'The only son of a businessman from Delhi. His father is one of those rags-to-riches cases. He is—he was very attractive…'

Mother interrupted, 'And tall and handsome, whether dark or fair never mattered to you, right? Okay, so he was a stereotype, but that alone would have been reason enough for you not to fall for him.'

'Maa, he had a sharp, ready wit too. He was a do-gooder,

and despite his affluence, he was not spoilt or immoral. He came from a noble family and he had genuine respect for women.'

Taking a deep breath, she continued, 'And don't forget, Maa, my singlehood was weighing on me. I was more than ready to take the plunge, provided Mr Right walked into my life. And that's what happened. I took the plunge, thinking that he was my Mr Right.'

Then she choked on her words, 'He was my first love, Maa. I believed what he said, but his betrayal lay in what he didn't tell me.'

Mother heaved a long sigh. She was realizing what her child had gone through. She knew that direct consolation would likely compound Bhanu's sense of loss, so she chose encouragement over sympathy, 'Bhanu, your name means the sun. There is an interesting context to your name that we have not told you so far. Your father and I had decided to have only one child, so that we could raise her or him in the best possible manner. Believe me, we thanked the Almighty a million times when you were born, because we both wanted a girl child. After that, it became our mission to bring you up in such a way that you would one day make us proud. On the sixth day of your birth, when the auspicious pooja was being performed for the welfare of the newborn child and the God of the sun was being invoked to bestow His divine favours on you, your father suddenly told me that you would be our son and sun. He said that you will light up our hearts and lives with your radiant qualities and trail-blazing achievements. That is why and how we named you Bhanu, our only son and sun. Let me tell you my child, you have never ever let us down. With you around, there has never been a cloudy day in our lives. We are proud of you. You are truly one in a million. Your break-up is a momentary setback like a partial solar eclipse. The sun can never be shadowed for long.'

Then mother hugged her daughter very tightly, letting her warmth convey that she shared her pain. When Bhanu felt better, she sought to lighten the moment, 'In all of your 21 years, you could not find love in Mumbai, and you pulled it off in less than 15 days in that barren, frigid, godforsaken place?'

Bhanu looked slightly offended at Mother's less-than-respectful reference to Zanskar, 'Mom, on its surface, Zanskar is barren, inhospitable and out-of-bounds, but that is only in maps and satellite images. The ground reality is different. It is those very negatives of Zanskar that make it so romantic and divine. All of us, without exception, found this trek a life-changing experience in some way or the other. An amateur photographer amongst us found a whole new way of looking at landscapes, and for the more earthy ones, it was the sheer challenge of surviving amidst such inconceivable hardships, which made them better men and women. Yet others found it glamorous, while the trek organizers felt that it offered them a new spiritual experience every time they went there. For me, it was first love through which I discovered Zanskar's true value. The environment, the ecology, the hardships, the people; they all taught me what true love is, and how fulfilling it can be without fast cars and fast food. I discovered there, how little one needs to be happily in love, provided one loved truly and unconditionally.'

Bhanu could be silver-tongued when inspired. Mother let her continue, 'In fact, I even told him that the Zanskar love was not about how much or what one had, but it was about how much one could share from whatever one had. Both of us were literally taken aback by how an apparently frigid ecology can change one's entire perspective on one of the most elementary human emotions—love. In short, Maa, Zanskar is the best place to fall in love, if you know what I mean.'

Mother marvelled at her daughter, 'Hmmmm, the Zanskar love, I like it, it has a nice ring to it, and it makes sense. I get you, the desert cactus blooms for longer than the rose in the pot. Okay, what happened then?'

'Then what maa, then love happened,' Bhanu said helplessly, 'That bastard showed me what love was and that place taught me how to love. I fell for him and gave him my commitment. He reciprocated in kind, and it became official.'

'So far so good. So where did it go wrong?'

Bhanu swallowed. The effort so far was telling on her face. She told her mother, 'Maa, what if we take a break?'

She replied, 'I understand. Dad is not in town. You will sleep in our room, in my lap.'

Bhanu extended her arms, 'Can't wait.'

Past midnight, her mother was woken up from a shallow sleep by muffled sounds. She opened her eyes and saw Bhanu turned away from her, head buried deep in her pillow, body in a foetal position, sounds of suppressed sobs escaping her tight grip over the pillow. Mother was devastated. She touched Bhanu's shoulders, then gently turned her to face her and said, 'Am I nobody to you that you decided to suffer alone?'

Bhanu lied, 'I did not want to disturb your sleep.'

The pain of separation is very acute in the quiet of late nights. Bhanu's pillow was drenched with her tears. She was gasping for air between muffled sobs. Is this the reward of loving? She thought and told her mother, 'Maa, I never want to love again.'

What could mother say to that? She placed her child's face in her lap and patted her forehead lovingly. Tears started streaming from her eyes and fell on Bhanu's face. It was a mother suffering the pain of her child. Only the bodies were separate, the pain was one.

Countless moments passed that way and mother's distress grew. Bhanu realized that she would have to at least pretend to be strong, or else Maa would slide deeper into anguish. She pulled herself up, cleared her throat and said, 'It's all right mom, let some time pass. I promise you I will bounce back. I will be fine, as good as new.'

Bhanu's mother's face was a crooked mask of pain and pride. She nodded and showed Bhanu a 'thumbs up' sign. Then she sang Bhanu's favourite lullaby and she drifted into sleep, but mother sat there motionless for a long time.

The next morning was like the calm after the storm. Mother and daughter shared breakfast from one plate. They chatted about what had happened while Bhanu was away, about the neighbour's dog having been hurt by a speeding car, and how proud the maid's daughter had made her by coming first in the final exams, and such small talk that helped keep serious matters at bay.

Around late morning, Bhanu asked mother if she had watched the latest Bollywood flick, and mother said no. They made it to the noon show. The screen displayed mesmerizing snowscapes in the opening shots, and Bhanu immediately related it with Zanskar. She nudged mother and told her in an excited, hushed tone, 'Look mom, that is so much like Zanskar. In fact, it can be easily mistaken for Zanskar.'

The monochrome, rugged, snowy mountainscape that covered the screen from edge to edge was indeed breathtaking. Mother whispered back, 'Hmmmm, pretty. Now I have to agree that Zanskar is the best place to fall in love.'

After the show, they snacked at Bhanu's favourite eatery before driving home. As the shadows lengthened, Bhanu felt much better. She told her mother, 'Mom, if it were you versus the rest of the world, I could do without the world.'

Mother said, 'Likewise,' and asked Bhanu to make coffee.

Settling over coffee, Bhanu picked up from where she had left off the previous evening, 'Mom, just when I had started living on cloud nine, the rug was pulled from under my feet.'

She narrated the Nerak incident fully but in pieces, 'A chill ran down my entire body and I felt as if I was being emptied from within, and that hollow space then started caving in. It was a strange feeling which I had never experienced before—I can't think of proper words for it, but at that moment I realized how badly a knockout punch would hurt.'

Bhanu crawled into her mother's lap, and she patted her forehead silently.

'The worst moment came when he admitted she was his fiancée. Although from their talk I could guess who she was, I needed him to tell me. I needed the man who I trusted blindly to tell me that he had indeed betrayed my trust.'

'Did you slap him?' Mother was momentarily overcome by a feeling of vengeance.

'I did more than that. I spat on his face.'

'Oh gosh, Bhanu! That's not like us!'

'Yes, I immediately regretted it. But Maa, there comes a time at least once in your life when you are so shocked and repulsed by the betrayal and injustice that nothing else but getting even would help you get over the hurt and humiliation. Besides, having done it, I could not have taken it back. So, I just walked away from him.'

Mother asked, 'Then?'

'Then I broke in parts. First, my body froze, then my heart blacked out, and finally, my brain conked off. I fell to the ground with what seemed like an earth-shattering thud. When I regained consciousness, we had already rejoined the main group. I was carried back on a stretcher given by the villagers. I had chosen to cut myself off from everybody and withdrawn into a shell. The only other person who gave me any comfort was a young Zanskari lady named Jigmet.'

Then she narrated her conversation with Jigmet—especially the part where she said that love was not water stored in a pot which could be turned on or off with a tap. Bhanu also told her mother the amazing fact that these ladies travelled as far as Leh on the frozen river to leave their children in a boarding school.

Mother was awestruck, 'Amazing!'

Bhanu nodded, then continued, 'By then I had forced myself to ignore his presence totally, as if he did not exist. His desperation to communicate with me grew by the hour. When we reached Delhi, he convinced one of the trek organizers to mediate and arrange a meeting between us. I could not refuse the organizer's pleas to at least listen to him, so I agreed reluctantly. In the meeting, he kept on rambling about how he loved me and did not want to lose me by telling about his engagement, and how he never wanted to cheat on me but was only waiting for an appropriate time to tell me about it. Then he went on to say that he would have ultimately pulled it off, he would have convinced his parents and his fiancée that the arranged alliance would not work, and that he wanted to spend his life with me. I then asked him what he would have done had he not succeed in convincing his parents and his fiancée. He tried to duck the question; he fumbled and remained evasive. I persisted with my query, and finally he conceded that in that case, "family first."'

Mother remained silent and let Bhanu complete her ordeal, 'Maa, I could not stand his sight anymore. I stood up and walked out of the coffee shop, picked up my belongings from the rest house and headed for the airport. Once I had secured a ticket, I called you to pick me up at the airport.'

Bhanu's eyes were lost. She let out a half-sob, 'Maa it's been said that you never love again like the first time. We had even decided on our children's names.'

Mother had no words. She continued to pat Bhanu's forehead absentmindedly. Sensing that mother was again slipping into deep sorrow, Bhanu had to regain her composure, 'But any way, whatever has happened, can't be undone. Life is not always fair. I have promised to you that I will get over it soon, and I will. I just need some time and you beside me.'

Bhanu's mother said, 'You have both, unconditionally.'

'Thanks Maa, I am proud to be your child.'

'I am proud you are my child.'

'Just one thing Maa, I won't be able to face Paa with this. Handle it your way with him.'

'Leave it to me. And you are spotless, my child. Don't ever feel small or smeared because of this.'

~

Dr Bhutia was shaken when he came to know of what had happened to Bhanu, but he was not the one to externalize his emotions. As was his habit while confronting complex, major issues, he listened to everything silently, and when it was over, he got up without saying a word and retired to his small library. He remained awake throughout the night, letting the matter sink in, absorbing the shock, and then working his way through the problem to develop a logical solution. When he came out from the library at pre-dawn, he saw that his wife was also awake. He asked for tea, and when it was ready, the couple settled down to talk. Dr Bhutia began, 'Ever since she was a child, we have taught Bhanu that life may seem unfair at times. But when the rough patch is crossed, the journey always leaves behind important lessons. We have taught her to face injustice with righteousness, perseverance and courage. However, no amount of good parenting can prepare a child to come out unscathed from heartbreak. All the good advice is reduced to mere theory when emotional catastrophe strikes a young woman. Bhanu is our own flesh and blood, and we know that, for all her boisterousness, she is very sensitive. This was the first major traumatic experience in life. We must focus on getting her out of it as soon as possible. I thought about it all night. What if we took a break and went to Gangtok? I think she needs a change of place above everything else. And even we have not visited our hometown for many years. I am sure Gangtok will do a world of good to her, and we will get our well-deserved break.'

Bhanu's mother immediately accepted the suggestion and talked to Bhanu over brunch. She, too, lapped up the idea. Memories of previous visits to Gangtok flooded her mind. The laidback chilly evenings on MG Road, the freshness of scented mountain air, the detoxing peace and quiet, the child-like innocence of townspeople, their easy becoming smiles and their capacity to enjoy life's small delights, the crunch of fresh snow under the feet—it all seemed therapeutic to Bhanu. She welcomed the idea excitedly, 'Maa, I cannot wait for this to happen!'

The Bhutia family left for Gangtok three days later.

6

The Hurt Heart Begins To Heal

Dr Bhutia's ancestral house in Gangtok overlooked the bustling M.G. Road. It had large rooms opening to wide verandas that ran through the façade of the building. They served as sit-outs and hubs for socializing, where small talk and gossip mingled with kinship among the residents. It was full of old-world charm where entire neighbourhoods lived like an extended family. One did not need to ring the bell or knock before entering the adjacent home.

Dr Bhutia had informed the residents in advance that they would be visiting. No sooner had the Bhutias arrived, than the building flocked to welcome them and exchange greetings, and to say that if anything was needed, they just had to ask for it. Invariably, each one of them had brought something for the Bhutias, either fresh snacks or a steaming drink or an entire meal. The welcome was so warm that the Bhutias instantly felt they belonged there. Two college-going girls came to 'give company' to Bhanu in the evening and chattered about all the 'happening things' in the town's campus life. After the elaborate narratives, they asked Bhanu how campus life in Mumbai was, and were left aghast at Bhanu's updates. 'So naughty, no?!' one girl exclaimed. Bhanu winked, 'Want to hear more?' The girl nodded sheepishly, and so Bhanu went on.

After tea and snacks, they took Bhanu out to M.G. Road. It was a neatly laid out road with potted flower beds adorning the road divider and unhurried people sitting on benches, waving at passers-by every other minute. At this time of the year, there were very few tourists. The idle shopkeepers killed time gossiping with anyone and everyone who came along. Bhanu, the college student from Mumbai, became an instant role model for youngsters. Some daring young boys even offered her ice cream, while one actually brought a chocolate bar and said, 'Let's share some sweetness.'

Bhanu smiled and accepted the bar, revelling in the attention she was getting. She took an instant liking to the young crowd. Of course, the boys were flirtatious, but their intentions were limited to making an impression on the girl from Mumbai. She found them charming in their clumsiness. The highlight of the evening was when a braggart told her that he had vacationed overseas the previous year. His friends gave him a puzzled look, since they had spent that entire vacation with him in Gangtok. When Bhanu asked him where he had been, he replied proudly that he had first gone to Berlin and then to Germany.

OMG! Bhanu was clean-bowled by that! It was like someone going to Delhi and then visiting India! She found the brag so comic that she decided to play along. Wearing an impressed look, she patted the space beside her on the bench and beckoned the author of the fiction to sit there. Thinking that he had pulled off a big one, the young lad seized the opportunity. Gloating, he looked at Bhanu as equals do. She looked back straight into his eyes and shaped her mouth in a donut-sized 'O', 'Oh, how wonderful! If I were the jealous type I could have easily envied you. I wish I was lucky enough to visit countries like Berlin and Germany, it's my dream!'

Then she blinked a few times in wonderment and wore a starry-eyed look, 'Tell me more about it, naa.'

The boy straightened and stiffened simultaneously, his lungs bursting with fresh oxygen and even more pride. He cleared his throat in self-importance before he spoke, 'Yeah, the atmosphere is so clean there and people don't do dirty things on streets like in India.' He rolled his r's and westernized his 'yeahs'.

Retaining her smitten look, Bhanu exclaimed, 'Oh so if they don't do dirty things on the streets, where do they do it, in the bathroom or in bedroom?'

The humour was lost on the young lad. He spread his arms Shah Rukh-style and continued, 'Oh yeah, they are very careful type, they don't throw papers or spit on roads. They don't even talk as loudly as we do.'

'How cultured!' Bhanu exclaimed.

And the boy nodded, 'Yeah, yeah.'

The small gathering around the bench was waiting with bated breaths for some flirting to begin, which, they presumed, was the only purpose of any talk between college-going boys and girls.

To fuel their curiosity, Bhanu moved closer to the boy and craned her neck as she spoke, making sure that he felt her breath on his face, 'All this sounds so interesting Mr…'

He blurted, 'Baldev.'

'Oh, Baldev, such a macho name, I love it. You know what Baldev, I am known for giving nice nicknames to people. For you, Baldie instantly came to my mind but you have such lovely, black hair on your handsome head. So ummmmm, yes, shall I make it Baddie, just for fun. You know, you are, in fact, very nice, but just for fun, you be my bad guy, Baddie.'

Baldev aka Baldie aka Baddie had never had such an

excitement-packed 10 minutes, so he bobbed his head with a stylish, 'Yeah, yeah.'

Bhanu pushed it, 'So Baddie, tell me which is the best place you liked in Berlin.'

Baddie said, 'Oh, in Berlin, there is this underground zoo.'

Bhanu was floored by that. She narrowed her eyes, 'Underground zoo?'

'Oh yeah, yeah, with big-big fishes swimming all around.'

'Oh, silly me! You mean a tunnel aquarium with big-big fishes swimming all around.'

Baddie nodded, 'Oh, yeah, yeah.'

'Okay. What about Germany?'

'In Germany, it was the Eiffel Tower which I liked the most. It is a world-famous, 1000-meter-high, metal pyramid. From the top you get a great view of entire Germany. We went right on the terrace and took snaps.'

Bhanu was stumped again. A pyramid-shaped Eiffel Tower in Germany was even more incredible than the underground zoo in Berlin.

She made sure she looked widely amazed before saying, 'Oh, Baddie I can't wait to see those snaps. Let's meet here tomorrow same time, what do you say?'

Baddie went from pink to pale instantly. He said non-committally, 'Oh yeah, sure.'

Bhanu looked at her watch and said, 'I hate to go now but I have to go. It was great meeting you Baddie. I had never imagined there will be a dashing guy like you in Gangtok. Well, Goodnight, Baddie.'

Bhanu extended her hand and Baddie kept shaking it for so long that Bhanu had to wriggle it out from his grip after a minute. The group began to disperse, wishing each other goodnight and saying 'see ya' with new-found western tongues. Bhanu had preserved her best move for the parting moment. After walking a few steps from Baddie, she turned around and said, 'Oh I meant to ask you Baddie, if you can give me your mobile number, perhaps we can chat a bit before going to sleep?'

Baddie screamed his phone number for the entire town to hear.

At ten in the night, Bhanu texted him.

—Gud nite Baddie, wonder why Im not able to sleep, mayb it's the cold.

Baddie replied in ten seconds.

—Gud nite Bhanu you r so sweet.

—Don't forget d snaps 2moro Im so excited to see them.

Baddie did not reply. Bhanu giggled and curled up beside her mother. She told her about the evening and Baddie, and about his international vacation in Berlin and Germany, and about the underground zoo and the pyramid-shaped Eiffel Tower. Mother smiled but then cautioned her, 'Don't you start your pranks here, Bhanu, this is Gangtok, not Mumbai.'

Bhanu said, 'At least I am starting something, Maa,' and turned away from her.

Bhanu was surprised to realize that for the first time, she had not thought about Bhushan for an entire evening. She was both relieved and pained at the thought—relieved because perhaps she was finally stepping out of her past, and pained because she still felt guilty when she did not think about him for even a short time. Was it that secretly, she still did not want to let go of him?

As the clock struck twelve, familiar memories returned to haunt her. Strangely, she was glad they did, as she felt out of place without their company, especially at night when sleep was hard to come by.

~

When Bhanu reached the hangout spot the following evening, the gang was already present in full strength. She greeted everybody a vivacious 'Hiiii' and sat beside Baddie with authority as if she belonged there. Baddie looked shifty, so she asked him, 'Helloooo, Mr Hottie, why so lukewarm today?'

Baddie replied, 'No, nothing, just having a bad headache.'

'Oww, poor boy, took some medicines?'

'I will take a pill if I am not okay by tonight.'

Then, to set minds wagging, she said sweetly, 'It was great chatting with you last night, Baddie. I must say that you are good at it.'

People's imaginations ran amok at the ambiguous 'at it.'

Baddie's face flushed, 'You're good at it too, Bhanu.'

She sounded appropriately relieved, 'Oh then, it's okay.'

Then Bhanu changed tracks abruptly, 'C'mon now, where are the pictures?'

Baddie fumbled, 'Err, what pictures?'

Bhanu, 'Arre, pictures, yaar, of your international holiday, the underground zoo and German Eiffel Tower.'

'Oh, that.'

'Yeah, that. C'mon, show me.'

Baddie came up with a half-baked lie, 'Actually, you know the photos are in mom's cupboard, and she has accidentally taken the keys with her—she has gone to Kolkata, you know.'

And one of the girls in the gang exclaimed, 'Oh how can that be? I met auntie at the mall today.'

That did Baddie in. Pale with embarrassment, he got up

to leave, but Bhanu pulled his sleeve and beckoned him to sit. She told him, 'Baddie, my friend, you need not have gone as far as Eiffel Tower in Germany to impress me. You are nice as a Gangtok guy. Be yourself; these days, girls prefer authentic guys.'

She patted his back understandingly and added, 'Tall claims don't impress me; good guys do.'

Colour returned on Baddie's face. He smiled gingerly and said, 'Sorry.'

Bhanu reassured him, 'It's okay. Peace.'

Then she said, 'Hey! Why don't you take me sightseeing? I hear there are many beautiful picnic spots here.'

And Baddie was his original enthusiastic Baldev again, 'Yeah sure, why not!'

The group went for three picnics the following week. Baddie pursued Bhanu all through those outings, but she played hard-to-get. He brought a lavish bouquet for her on the morning of the first picnic, but she said she would have preferred something spontaneous and original like a purple wild-flower with a slender stem. He tried to be more spontaneous and original the next time, but it proved too literal; Bhanu burst out laughing at his gift of a cookbook. She had never cooked even rice. Desperate to come up with a winner for the third picnic, he consulted his friends, and the collective decision fell on a beautiful multi-coloured bead necklace with wool tassels. Bhanu fell for it but decided to be a snob, 'Ummm, okay. But did you make it yourself?'

Taken aback, Baddie replied in the negative; just as she had never cooked anything, he had never stitched a button.

'I like to receive self-made gifts; this is so impersonal, you know.'

Baddie bobbed his head.

'So start learning how to make necklaces, Baddie.'
Baddie bobbed his head again.
And Bhanu burst out laughing.

~

The first ten days in Gangtok had a calming effect on Bhanu. Her days were spaced out, and her new friends' company was fun. In particular, she had formed a liking for the good boy, Baddie. His naiveté was charming. Even his made-up vacation stories were amusing to Bhanu. She found that his bragging spoke of his inner desire to achieve what seemed out of reach for him. He was straightforward and uncomplicated in a likeable, small-town way. He was not very intelligent, but that let him think from the heart. And he was good-looking—broad-shouldered, naturally ruddy and strong, tall, with a freckled face, small eyes and a boyish grin. He was not groomed in mannerisms; he would not even know how to hold the door for a girl, but he was large-hearted and always there for friends when needed. On the whole, Bhanu thought that he was a good package, and so she continued to flirt with him.

However, as far as Baddie was concerned, it was for the first time that any girl was getting close to him. He was smitten by Bhanu and was getting serious about her. When she realized that her behaviour was sending wrong signals to Baddie, she decided to set things straight. One night, she called up Baddie, and he jumped out of his bed with excitement. A call from Bhanu at that hour instead of her usual texts! That was some progress! Mustering all the excitement in his voice, he tried to start the conversation humorously, 'Hi Bhanu! It's so great to hear your sweet voice after ages!'

'Baddie, we met just a few hours ago.'

'Feels like ages to me'

'Not at this end,' Bhanu quipped and added, 'Baddie, I want to talk.'

Baddie was concerned by Bhanu's uncharacteristically serious tone, 'You sound serious. Everything okay, Bhanu?'

'Yes, so far. And I want things to be okay, that's why I called.'

Now she had Baddie's rapt attention.

She came to the point, 'Okay, if you think our friendship can develop into anything more serious, then you are mistaken. There simply is no scope.'

That brought Baddie down to the earth. He asked, 'You are already committed to someone?'

'I live in the present, Baddie. I am single and not ready to mingle.'

'But why?'

'My choice.'

The moment she said that, she realized it was a bit harsh on Baddie. Besides, she reckoned that rejection, whether of self or others, should always be handled with care. She tried to be tactful with her next line, 'Baddie, we hit it off wonderfully as friends, so let it be just friendship.'

But Baddie persisted, 'Look, Bhanu, I like you very much and want you in my life…'

Bhanu interrupted, 'Baddie, it's also about whether *I* want anybody in my life or not. As I said before, let's just be friends.'

Baddie swallowed. He asked after a moment, 'So, what now?'

Bhanu understood what Baddie was going through. Having made her point, she spoke more comfortingly, 'Baddie, you are handsome and very likeable. Only a fool like me can let go of you. You have a heart of gold. I am sure any girl would be lucky to have you.'

Baddie surprised Bhanu with his ready acceptance of reality. She liked him more for that—no drama, no scenes, he made it so simple and sporty, 'Well, okay. Love cannot be one-sided. Promise me that you will be my best friend.'

'I promise, Baddie. I'd love to be your BFF. Now smile, or I will take back my promise.'

Baddie texted a smiley to Bhanu and she lapped it up, 'Hey I have an idea my latest BFF.'

'What?'

'From now onwards, you are Buddy, not Baddie.'

Baddie aka Buddy flushed, 'You are impossible, Bhanu.'

'Thanks. So Buddy, let's meet up tomorrow morning, just you and I, to celebrate our BFF. status.'

Next morning, the BFFs bonded over three hours of non-stop banter and mischief. Their friendship became stronger, and they started enjoying each other's companionship without any other expectations.

For Bhanu's parents too, Gangtok was a welcome change. It provided them rest, rejuvenation and reflection, all of which was a luxury in the hectic Mumbai life. However, Dr Bhutia was required to start another lecture tour soon, so their time in Gangtok was limited. The couple talked it out with Bhanu, who was reluctant to leave Gangtok. She told them, 'Paa, Maa, I like it here. The place and the friends I have made here are helping me heal. In Mumbai, I will be alone, with no company and nothing to do. My friends there will not have the time and inclination to be with me constantly. Here, I have Buddy. I want to stay longer.'

Bhanu's parents could not agree more. Mother said, 'Feel free to stay here as long as you wish, beta. We will leave on Sunday.'

Bhanu invited Buddy for lunch on the day before her parents

were to leave. He presented himself in brand new clothes and a fresh haircut. Bhanu poked a finger in his belly as she opened the door, 'Hey stranger! Do I know you?'

Buddy extended his hand but Bhanu took him in her arms instead. 'Come,' she said warmly and introduced him to her parents. They chatted in a casual and relaxed manner. Bhanu's poking humour added to the light-heartedness. When Dr Bhutia asked Buddy about his interests, Bhanu replied on his behalf, 'Girls,' and when her mother invited him to Mumbai, she said, 'Don't try your flirty ways there or you'll be in trouble.'

The parents left the two friends to themselves after lunch. Bhanu showed Buddy her college pictures and introduced her friends to him. He was awed by everything, from girls' curls to guys' abs. They talked endlessly until the evening chill set in and Buddy got up to go. Bhanu's parents came out to see him off. Mother said, 'Take care of Bhanu, Buddy. And call me if she gets out of control with her pranks.'

Buddy smiled, 'Yes, aunty.'

Next day, Bhanu and Buddy travelled up to Bagdogra from where the Bhutia couple was to fly to Kolkata. When the flight was announced, Bhanu hugged her parents and said, 'I will miss you Paa, Maa. Promise me to call and email every day.'

The parents promised, 'We will miss you too beta. Take care.'

Mother added, 'Eat properly and don't miss your daily supplements.'

Bhanu mocked annoyance, 'Mother, stop mothering me.'

But can mothers ever stop doing that?

~

Bhanu's parents kept their promise of daily contact. A week later, she received an email from Dr Bhutia. The subject line said, 'Sun-derella.' Intrigued, she opened the email immediately.

Bhanu,

We can't say this enough—you are our sun and son. After receiving you, we have never asked for anything from the Almighty. You are all we ever wanted.

Cinderella was your favourite fairy tale as a child. As we watched you grow up, we saw the fairy come alive all around us. In you, we see her beauty and kindness, her courage and generosity. You fill our hearts and our home with her radiant energy. And your boisterous laughter and cheer are like sunrays on fertile soil. They make our lives fuller and richer.

Bhanu, you are more than Cinderella to us, you are our Sun-derella.

You are the light of our lives.

Maa and Paa

Those words melted Bhanu like how warmth melts ice. She immediately called home.
'Maa.'
'Oh Bhanu, I knew it would be you.'
'I read the email.'
'And? Did you like the fairy tale?'
'It was crap.'
'Oh! Are we that bad storytellers?'
'The worst.'
'Why?'
'Fairy tales bring a smile, not tears.'
'I am sure they were tears of joy.'
And Bhanu began crying some more.

When she was done, she said, 'Maa, you are the best mom on earth.'

'And Paa?

'Super-cool. Super-dad.'

'I...we...', a knot formed in her mother's throat and she could not speak.

Bhanu let a few moments pass, and then said, 'Maa you'll have to marry dad for seven lives'

Mother found her voice, 'Why?'

'Cause I want to be born as your child that many times.'

Then she ended the call abruptly, 'Bye maa.' Immediately, Bhanu punched Buddy's number.

'Where are you?' she said when he answered her call.

'At home, why?'

'Come here right away'

'Why? what happened, Bhanu?' Buddy was worried.

'Buddy please, no questions, come right away'

He made it in record time. The moment she closed the door behind him, she lent her entire weight on him and cried. Buddy was too dazed to respond in any way, so he just stood there, leaning against the wall.

After a while, she raised her face and asked, 'You want to know why I could not be your girlfriend?'

'I can guess, but tell me.'

'I am still recovering from a fractured heart, and it is not fair to give someone something broken. In fact, the purpose of coming to Gangtok was to help me overcome the split.'

'I hope it helped.'

'It did, more than you can imagine. Especially, having you as my friend.'

Then she released him and said, 'Sit. Tea?'

'Yes.'

Over tea, she told him all about Zanskar and thereafter. Then she showed him her parents' email and said, 'Paa and Maa, they are my pillars of strength. And you too Buddy, thank you for being my BFF.'

In reply, Buddy asked Bhanu to get up. It was the first time he had said anything to Bhanu with such authority. There was a strange glint in his eyes. Bhanu got up. Without warning, he wrapped her in a passionate embrace. In unguarded moments, raw passion overtook friendship. Friendly warmth soon turned into the heat of lust. The need for companionship turned into desire, and friends became woman and man, wanting each other badly, blindly. Buddy lifted Bhanu and tossed her on the bed, then mounted her and began kissing her hard.

Whatever it was that caused desire to get the better of friendship—the emotionally charged atmosphere, or their irresistible fondness for each other, or something else—whatever it was, it breached the sanctity of their friendship, until reasoning returned as suddenly as it had left them. Bhanu was the first to come out of the spell. She tried to push Buddy off herself and when he resisted, she said edgily, 'Let go of me Buddy.'

'Why?'

'Why??? Damnit, Buddy, because it's not done between friends. Because it's so uncool. Only cowards do it under the guise of friendship.'

'We could be more than friends, Bhanu.'

'*No. Never.* I have told you before, it's not to be. Don't you realize that I am not yet emotionally capable of it? Besides, we are friendship material, Buddy. Whatever just happened was temporary madness. It never happened, okay? I am a bit fussy about sex. Whenever I do it, whoever I do it with—and I don't care if he is or isn't my husband—I want it to be 110 per cent. I want to give it my 110 per cent, drenched in emotion and commitment. I want to do it with my soulmate. The last person I want sex with is my best friend.'

By then, Bhanu had got off the bed. She gathered herself, sat on a chair, and asked Buddy to sit on the chair facing her and continued, 'You are a godsend, Buddy. I value our wonderful friendship very much. It's above momentary temptations. Believe me, it's hard for me to resist your warm embrace, to let go of the feel of your strong arms. But that's prescription for disaster. Let's forget that this ever happened. I love you, as a friend. Period.'

Buddy smiled tentatively at Bhanu, embarrassment written all over his face, and got up to leave, 'I have to go now.'

She patted his back gently, 'Thank you for understanding.'

After that accidental intimacy, their friendship was on a roll. Bhanu managed to keep Buddy in a cosy comfort zone but at arm's length. Buddy knew that the boundary was drawn, and went by the rulebook.

7
Tragedy Strikes Suddenly

Late one night, Bhanu was disturbed by the persistent ringing of her mobile phone. She took the call still half sleep, but woke up with a start when she heard her mother's voice, 'Mum! It's three in the night. I hope everything is okay'

'Hi Beta sorry to call at this hour, but dad is unwell.'

Bhanu's thoughts went berserk, 'Why, what happened, Maa?'

'Dad has suffered a heart attack. His blood pressure was unusually high after he returned from the lecture tour. I insisted we visit the doctor immediately but he did not, saying that it was just travel fatigue. Then today, he suddenly complained of chest pain after dinner. We immediately rushed to the hospital…'

Bhanu was edgy, 'Paa is in the intensive coronary care unit?'

'Well, yes.'

She got angry, 'What took you so long to inform me?'

'Listen, I had to manage a hundred things all by myself…'

'Cut the crap Maa, you could have asked someone to inform me if you were so occupied. Then she said, 'I will leave Gangtok tomorrow and come down to Mumbai.'

'Give me a call when you reach Mumbai.'

Bhanu said, 'I will' and cut the call abruptly. She regretted it immediately, and called back, 'Sorry, Maa, I realize what you would be going through right now. But don't worry. We will overcome this. Nothing will happen to Paa, I promise.'

For once, mother needed daughter's shoulders to lean on, 'I need you. Come soon.'

'Don't worry, Maa. I am coming.'

~

Bhanu tried to sleep but gave up after a while, and busied herself with packing up. At six, she called Buddy, 'Hi Buddy! Good morning.'

Buddy was used to Bhanu's ill-timed calls by then, so he just mumbled sleepily, 'Good morning.'

'Buddy, Mom called me at 3:00 a.m., Paa is unwell.'

That woke him up instantly, 'Oh, what happened?'

'Paa has had a heart attack and is in the ICCU. I am leaving tomorrow—I mean today.'

'I am coming,' Buddy said without blinking.

She said, 'No, it's okay,' but immediately realized that he could be of much help, 'Actually, I wish I had a brother to depend on at such times.'

'I will come as soon as I can.'

'Perfect.'

'Tell you what, Bhanu? I will pick you up at eight. We will have breakfast at my home and then leave for Bagdogra.'

'Sounds great. Okay then, waiting' Bhanu said, and ended the call.

Breakfast was quiet; the upsetting news weighed heavily on everyone. Bhanu bowed to Buddy's parents before leaving and said, 'Uncle, Aunty, I am at a loss of words to express my gratitude to you all. I will just say that I missed my parents and my home less because of you all.'

Buddy's mother replied, 'Oh, don't say that Bhanu, we have

always wanted a daughter, and we have found her in you.'

Buddy's father added, 'Consider our home yours and do come again.'

Buddy's father blessed Bhanu as she left, 'Go safely, beti. We will pray for your father's speedy recovery. And I hope Baldev is of help to you."'

The travel from Gangtok to Bagdogra and the flight to Delhi were quiet. Bhanu was too anxious to speak, so Buddy left her alone with her thoughts. There was an hour's wait at the Delhi airport before they could check-in for the flight to Mumbai. Bhanu could not help reminiscing the last time she was there—the same terminal, the same flight to Mumbai, the same waiting period—was it just a few months back? She shuddered at the thought.

They went straight to the hospital after landing. Bhanu hugged her mother tightly, 'How are you, Maa?'

Mother deflected the question, 'I'm so relieved you are here.'

Then Buddy bowed to her and said, 'How are you, Aunty? I am sorry to hear about Uncle's illness.'

Mother took him in her arms, 'Baldev, thank you for coming. You will be of tremendous help.'

Then Bhanu asked her impatiently, 'How is Paa? What have the doctors said?'

Mother said, 'There are five blockages. Looking at his diabetic condition and the number of blockages, they have opted for bypass surgery tomorrow.'

Bhanu looked at her father from the glass window of the ICCU. The massive cardiac arrest had left him very weak; he was lying in bed awake but inert. Bhanu was shocked to see him that way. She asked mother, 'Can I pop in?'

'Yes, but make it brief and don't cause any stress to him.'

Bhanu tip-toed into the ICCU. Dr Bhutia was a strong man of sterling character. And now, seeing her father so hapless, a network of tubes going in and out of his body, so helplessly at the mercy of external life aids, shook Bhanu to the core. He looked as though he had aged many years in the last couple of days. However, she maintained her poise as she took a few steps towards him. Dr Bhutia managed a weary smile at her. She sat on the chair beside the bed and grinned broadly, 'My daddy strongest!'

That was Bhanu's favourite childhood line when her father used to lift her up on his shoulders and dance all around the house.Dr Bhutia had no strength to speak. His face remained impassive, as if not agreeing with her. She moved her hand soothingly over his forehead, 'I mean it, Dad. You are my Superman. This heart-attack is nothing. You will soon be out of here.'

Dr Bhutia tried to utter something, but Bhanu immediately stopped him, 'Sssshhhh, my Superman, you are in silent mode.'

Then she took his hand in hers, closed her eyes and said a silent prayer. She tried to concentrate all the positive energy within her and transmitted it to him. After a while, she opened her eyes, 'Done. I declare you cured!' and gave that silly smile her father adored.

Before leaving, she patted his forehead again and said confidently, 'Paa, you will be in and out of the surgery within no time. Don't worry. God is with us.'

Although he was properly covered with the quilt, Bhanu adjusted its folds before leaving as if to console herself that there was something she could do for him.

The hospital allowed only one person to stay with the patient during the night. After a debate, it was decided that her mother and Buddy would go home, and Bhanu would remain with Dr Bhutia. As they were leaving, Bhanu's mother complained, 'This is not fair. You have hardly slept last night and have had a long day flying between cities, and now, a wakeful night on top of it.'

Bhanu sounded annoyed, 'Maa, did you keep a count of the sleepless nights you and Paa spent, just to make sure I did not doze off while studying? Now go, I am fine. Buddy, Good night.'

~

The surgery was scheduled for 10:00 a.m. the next day. During the night, Bhanu researched the risk factors of diabetic patients undergoing bypass surgery. Realizing that it was a high-risk surgery, she had noted several points of discussion with the doctors. She requested a pre-operation interview with the surgeon in the morning. While she was busy reading about the surgical procedure and double-checking on matters like arrangement for blood, Mrs Bhutia handled phone calls on three mobile phones, which kept on ringing continuously, often together. There was a deluge of concern and worry among relatives, friends, colleagues and well-wishers as the news of Dr Bhutia's hospitalization spread. Many of them offered to be present during the surgery. Mrs Bhutia courteously but firmly kept the crowd away. On the other hand, Buddy proved to be a true friend in need, ceaselessly doing errands.

Dr Bhutia was allowed a couple of minutes to be with his wife and daughter before the surgery. He was aware that he might not survive the surgery. He folded his hands and looked at his wife and Bhanu as if bidding them a final adieu. Mrs Bhutia felt crushed by the weight of the moment. She slowed down to trail behind her husband's gurney, or else he would have noticed her welling eyes. Bhanu, however, braved a smile,

'Hey Superman, you will overcome this, you will be fine.'

He tried to say something, but Bhanu quickly preempted him, 'Ssshhh, Superman, you are in silent mode.'

And despite the gravity of the situation, Dr Bhutia's face creased in a weak smile. Then, he was wheeled into the operation theatre, and the red light above the door went on.

The torturous wait began.

~

At half-past nine, a nurse came rushing out of the operation theatre and issued frantic instructions to the front office for additional blood supply. Bhanu lunged at the nurse before she could vanish behind the door and asked, 'What's the matter, Sister?'

'There is some bleeding, and he will need to undergo another transfusion, but nothing to worry about.' She left it at that and went back into the operating room.

All colour drained from Bhanu's face. Her research the previous night said that excessive bleeding during coronary bypass surgeries was a major complication. Her mother tugged at her sleeve frantically and asked, 'What's the matter, Bhanu? We had arranged for enough blood. Why this sudden need for more blood? What does it mean?'

Bhanu had to make an enormous effort not to sound panicked, 'Maa, at times the patient bleeds a little more than expected during the surgery, that's all. Believe me; there is no danger to Paa.'

Mother sounded frustrated, 'Oh, that's what the nurse also said. Tell me honestly, is there any danger?'

'No, Mum. Trust me, Paa is going to be all right.'

Buddy walked up to Bhanu and asked the same thing,

and she gave him the same answer. Inwardly, though, she was coming apart. For a moment, she wished she had not researched the procedure the previous night; sometimes, ignorance meant bliss. She started pacing the corridor and tried to ward off ill-boding thoughts from her mind. The Bhutia family did not observe rituals, but for once, Bhanu wished she knew chants that could de-stress and mantras that could provide relief to suffering mortals. Buddy came to her and put a hand around her shoulders, saying, 'Bhanu, God is with us. Don't worry.'

She looked at him and nodded in grateful acknowledgement.

Then they joined her mother, who was standing at the far end of the corridor.

At 10:40 a.m., the red light above the operation theatre door went off, and within minutes, Dr Bhutia's stretcher was wheeled out. The cardiac surgeon approached Mrs Bhutia and Bhanu. As he removed his face mask to speak, his grave, unsmiling face alarmed both of them. Defeat and dejection were evident in his voice as he spoke in a soft, apologetic tone, 'I am sorry the surgery failed. We tried our best to arrest the heart attack that occurred in the middle of the surgery, but our efforts did not succeed. I knew Dr Bhutia personally. My heartfelt condolences.'

As the surgeon turned to leave, his shoulders stooped. His slumped stride seemed to convey that every loss of life is a personal loss for doctors.

In an instant, the world around the Bhutia family crumbled. Bhanu was the first to cave in. She had never cried vocally, and she did not do so even then. However, her face was twitched, distorted. She pressed her lips but could not prevent sobs from escaping sporadically. She slumped over her mother's shoulders and held her tightly, not wanting to let go of her. Surprisingly, Mrs Bhutia remained stoic, or so it seemed in the moments after the tragic news was conveyed. Maybe her overwhelming grief acted as anaesthesia, blocking all her capacity to feel. The pain would perhaps invade her later once the initial numbness was gone. Mother guided Bhanu to a row of empty seats. The daughter could not stop her tears, resting her face on her mother's shoulders, and after a while, collapsing in her lap. Long minutes passed, but neither of them spoke a word. Sometimes, silence and lack of communication give dignity to grief. Buddy came and sat beside them. He was a young man who had never encountered death. He was shaken and disoriented by the sudden development. He simply could not comprehend that life could snatch away a dear one so swiftly. His inexperience made his efforts to comfort Bhanu and her mother, rather clumsy. He did not know what to say.

A hospital staff member came and stood at a respectable distance until he was noticed by Bhanu. Her eyes were red and swollen by then, but she managed to pull herself up and nudged her mother to draw her attention to that person. He came to them and coughed lightly, then said, 'My heartfelt condolences. There are a few formalities to be completed to enable us to hand over the dead body.'

Dead body! It sounded so callous, yet so correct. What remains in a body after life departs? The corpse lying on the stretcher was not Dr Bhutia anymore.

Bhanu nodded to the hospital staff and signed on a few dotted lines to take charge of her father's corpse. Then she asked mother, 'What now, Maa? What next?' She sounded utterly lost.

Bhanu's mother had to put up a brave face, for Bhanu's sake, 'When life takes away something from you permanently, it also teaches you how to live without it.'

Bhanu nodded unconvincingly.

By then, friends and relatives had started streaming to the hospital. One of them said gently, 'The cremation will have to be completed by 6:00 p.m. The ambulance is ready. We must go home now.'

~

A large gathering had already assembled at home by the time the ambulance drove in. Dr Bhutia's body was placed in the anteroom for people to pay their last respects. The cremation march began around half-past three. Beating the social diktat, both Bhanu and Mrs Bhutia went to the cremation ground. Bhanu performed her father's last rites and lit the funeral pyre. Mrs Bhutia stood by and watched beyond the flames unblinkingly, her face solemn and her posture erect. Her vision was blurred by the smoke from the fire and the tears in her eyes, but there was a certain dignity in her grief. She did not seem like a person who had surrendered to destiny's cruel twist. She refused to break down as her husband's mortal remains were consumed by the holy fire.

Like her mother, Bhanu remained a proud daughter as the raging fire engulfed her father.

After the cremation, Bhanu and Mrs Bhutia talked to a few close relatives and announced that the prayer meeting would be held the next day at 4:30 p.m.

They reached home around eight. Buddy called his parents to convey the tragic news and tell them that he would stay back for a few days.

~

Around eleven, the household fell silent. Bhanu took her mother to her room to retire; her own room was too full of memories for her to retire.

Finally, alone, Mrs Bhutia let loose her repressed anguish. She collapsed on the bed and let out a low, wailing sound, repeatedly taking her husband's name between sobs. Bhanu tried to console her, 'Maa, please try to control your grief. If you break down, what will happen to me?'

Mother said, 'I feel like we have both become orphans.'

It is true. The loss of a caring husband can make a wife feel orphaned, apart from the children. Dr Bhutia had never been very vocal with his affections, but he had always taken care of all his family's wishes, even before they became needs. In the later years of a marriage, such a loving and responsible husband easily transforms into a fatherly figure.

Bhanu realized that it was necessary to let her mother vent her grief. She waited out those moments, gently patting her mother. When the tide had ebbed, she handed her mother a glass of water and said, 'Maa, our lives without Paa begin from tonight. He would hate it if we succumbed to grief and let it break us. He would rather we derive strength from his memories than let them weaken us. Tonight is our first fight in a long struggle, and we must win; Paa is watching from above. Let us make him proud. We will learn to carry on without Paa; we will manage somehow. I depend on you a lot. Let us be each other's strength.'

It was almost like mother and daughter had switched roles. Bhanu's mother replied, 'It is easier said than done, Bhanu.'

'I know Maa, but nothing is going to be easy now onwards.'

They hugged, lending each other their support.

Buddy brought warm milk for them and said, 'Please drink some milk.'

Bhanu took both the glasses gratefully and handed one to her mother.

Then looking at Buddy, she said, 'Buddy, my dearest friend, even the thought of saying thanks to you makes me feel small. I wonder if I deserve your friendship. I hope one day I can reciprocate what you are doing for us.'

Buddy began to say something, but Bhanu stopped him, 'All my Mumbai friends have left. Even my childhood buddies, my 2-a.m. friends, have not lasted beyond eleven. And you, Buddy, someone from thousands of kilometres away, who has barely known me for two months, to whom we are nobody, you did not think twice before compromising your studies to be with us at this time. You did it out of choice, not compulsion, just to help us, without any expectation! I can't even begin to think what choice I would have made in your place, and that's what makes me feel small in front of you…'

Buddy was not used to such a refined way of expressing one's thoughts. He sat there awkwardly, listening to Bhanu, 'Buddy, you are neither family nor a relative, yet you decided to be with us as if we are family…'

Then it was Buddy who interrupted Bhanu. He said simply, 'Bhanu, I only know that friends and family are not two very different things. And one more thing, in our family we believe that to be able to help somebody is our good luck, not theirs. We are just being the medium of help that is coming from above. So please don't say thanks. I am grateful to God that I am able to be here at this time.'

Bhanu and her mother were overwhelmed. Mother just said, 'Bhanu is right. We pray that someday we are able to give back to you in gratitude.'

Buddy said, 'I am like your son, Auntyji, and how can a

son do favours for a mother? Please finish your milk. And I am awake in the next room. Call me if you need anything.'

After he left, Bhanu asked her mother disbelievingly, 'Is he for real Maa?'

'Bhanu, no matter what, never let any harm come to this friendship. He is Almighty's manifestation.'

To that, Bhanu replied, 'Or has Paa sent him? You know, he was always good at planning for unforeseen emergencies.'

It was already midnight, but sleep was out of the question for both of them. Bhanu's mother remembered something Dr Bhutia had told her a few days before he was hospitalized, 'Your father was deeply worried for you ever since you came back from Zanskar. He would ask about you every night when we were alone. He knew very well that there are some things which a young daughter can share only with her mother, especially matters related to the heart. One night, he surprised me when he asked whether I had started preparing for your marriage. I was taken aback; we had decided never to pressure you into getting married. I told him that the question was totally out of context; you were in your college years and there was still a lot of time. At that, he sounded a little exasperated, "Where is the time?" I could not understand at that time, but now I realize that perhaps he had a premonition. It is said that people who are very pure at heart do have such intuitions. Anyway, he asked me to get the white silk sari with the flaming-red, embroidered pallu he had gifted me last Diwali. I thought he was in a romantic mood and wanted me to wear that sari and take me out for a late-night drive—he liked to spring such surprises at times.

'Nevertheless, I pretended to be puzzled and asked him why all that drama, and he said, "Just bring that sari." When I brought it, he looked at it with a strange, far-away look in his eyes and said, "Will you do me a favour?" I had not noticed the glint in his eyes and asked him back, "Will you do me a favour, Mr Husband? I can't manage to wear this heavy sari on my own; why don't you help me out?" Then I looked at his face. His forlorn eyes took me by surprise. I asked him what the matter was, and he said, "Nothing. Gift this sari to Bhanu when she gets married." Before I could react, he removed the ring that I had gifted him the same Diwali, put it in my palm, and said, "This is for our son-in-law." Now I was genuinely puzzled at his ill-timed concern for your marriage and told him in a lightly reprimanding tone to stop his stupidity. He replied, "I just want our happiness to pass on to them through these gifts." I said, "I understand your feelings, but isn't it too premature? It will be at least another five years before Bhanu gets married. By then, we would have given each other many more gifts, so if you want to do it your way and gift them second-hand stuff, why not choose from those gifts? They would be more contemporary too." He said, "Parents' feelings for their children never go out of fashion," and hugged me tightly for a long time. When he released me, he looked up toward the ceiling and beyond for a second, then his gaze settled on my face. But I did not miss that moment when he had looked upwards. It was as if he was conveying to the heavens that he had done his bit. Then he took me out for a drive and coffee. It was our last outing.'

Bhanu was flooded with emotions. What child would not be proud of such parents? And now, she was left with only her mother. The thought made her miss her father all the more. 'My daddy strongest, you have left me heartbroken' she rued, 'Maa, I don't know who I will marry if at all I ever do. But if I marry, I promise to pass on those priceless gifts to our child and will ask do the same. In that manner, the love story of Mrs and Dr Bhutia will live on.'

Both mother and daughter spent the night talking about Dr Bhutia. When one became slightly weak, the other became strong, so the night passed.

At dawn, they drifted into a shallow slumber, only to be woken up by a gentle knock on the door around seven. Buddy entered, wished them good morning and showed them Dr Bhutia's obituary in the newspaper.

Mrs Bhutia ran her fingers over the photograph, desperate to hold his face in her hands one last time. Bhanu sensed that her mother felt that the dawn had not brought them hope. She said, 'Maa, the first day without Paa will be equally challenging as the first night. And we have to be strong for each other.'

Mother nodded, and they got out of the room to face the day.

The prayer meeting was held between four and six in the evening. Visitors kept coming and going. Mumbai's intelligentsia, historians, and literati flocked the venue along with family, friends and relatives. By far, the most genuine sense of loss was reflected on the faces of Dr Bhutia's students. One of them even commented to Bhanu that he had lost not a teacher but a father and a mentor.

The crowd began to thin by seven. As was the custom, Bhanu, the child, was asked to speak a few words about Dr Bhutia. She got up, a proud daughter paying homage to her father, 'Respected elders and dear family, friends and well-wishers, Thank you for coming and sharing our grief. The value of human warmth and comfort is best understood by those who don't have the support of compassionate people at a time of momentous loss.

'Talking in the past tense about my father seems terribly unfair to him. Just before he was wheeled into the operation theatre, he had promised me that he would return unscathed. And he has always been true to his word. So, although Paa has lost his physical form, I am not ready to believe that he is not around. I know you are here, Paa, so a big hug to you with our favourite line, "My Daddy Strongest".'

Her voice cracked for a split second, but she quickly composed herself, 'I—ehm, we love you Paa, and we miss you. I have written a small note for you, just as I used to write when you were away on your lecture tours.'

Then, looking up at the skies, Bhanu unfolded a paper and began reading, 'Paa, Santa comes just once a year, during the Christmas season, but you are my all-season Santa. You are a giver who has always given unconditionally, a provider who knew what I needed even before I wanted it. Paa, you always loved me boundlessly, but never let excesses spoil me. You gave me freedom of chocie, but corrected me whenever I chose wrongly. You guided me through difficulties and dilemmas, but never thrust your views on me. You were always attentive, but never intrusive. You gave me wings to soar high, but also kept me grounded in values and principles. You taught me how to be independent without being irreverent, and confident without being rude…'

At that moment, Bhanu's hands began to tremble and her voice trailed off. Unable to continue the eulogy, she put the note back in her pocket, fighting back the stinging tears in her eyes. She concluded suddenly, 'Paa, you have given me my name—the sun. I will try to live up to that name. Keep guiding me always.'

There was a soft applause. Bhanu folded her hands and sat down.

The meeting dispersed around seven. After a light dinner, Bhanu took her mother to her room and they spent the night fondly remembering Dr Bhutia.

8

Life After Loss and More Twists and Turns

A week passed by. Bhanu had not accessed her email since her father had passed away so when she opened her inbox, a bagful of mails flooded her screen. Most of them were condolence messages, to which Bhanu copied and pasted a standard reply. As she scrolled down the inbox, one email caught her eye. The sender had flagged it as urgent and important, and in the subject line, they had written, 'B.P.S. is no more.' Bhanu frowned; she did not know anybody who bore those initials. She was about to delete the email, when her eyes fell on the sender's name—Bhushan B.P.S. She froze, her eyes fixed on the screen. After a while, she straightened a bit and opened the mail. It read like a bulk message:

> With profound grief, the B.P.S. family shares the tragic news of the demise of the late Shri Bhanu Pratap Singh in Delhi. The end came due to multiple organ failures in his unconscious state of mind.
>
> May his soul rest in peace.
>
> In deep mourning,
> Bhushan B.P.S. and family

Still transfixed, she read the email again and again. A little voice inside her screamed, 'The date! Look at the date!'

She checked the date of the demise and her mind went into a tizzy again. Both their fathers had departed on the same day. She had a wild thought: would they meet in the heavens by chance, and would they mention that he had a son, and he, a daughter, and his name was Bhushan and hers, Bhanu? Would the fathers bring them face-to-face again, that way?

She shuddered and shut down her laptop, leaving half of her emails unchecked.

When she signed in to her mailbox the next morning, Bhanu found a new email from Bhushan. The subject line read, Zanskar. She wanted to open the email instantly but resisted the temptation, thinking, what more could he want to say? Did she want to walk into that ruse again? *No!* she chided herself, and deleted the email.

However, she typed out a short reply to the first one, 'Our heartfelt condolences and prayers for the welfare of the departed soul.'

Visitors kept Bhanu, and her mother occupied throughout the day. In the evening, the two of them, along with Buddy, visited Bhanu's favourite eatery. Bhanu remembered how she would end up eating her father's share of her favourite, nachos-chaat, and he would have to order another plate every single time they went. A fond smile spread on her face as she recalled that incident to Buddy. While they were driving back, Bhanu asked her mother, 'Maa, I was surprised that I was not sad while remembering Paa at the eatery. Like, I remembered him without missing him.'

She felt slightly guilty, 'A few days, is that all that it takes not to miss one's Paa?'

Mother smiled understandingly. By then, she had regained her hold on herself. She said, 'You equate missing someone with being sad in their memory, but it is possible to live with someone's memories without letting them cause pain, especially if that someone was as loving and caring as your father. That's how I have reconciled with reality. I have promised myself not to live in sorrow; that would pain his soul as much as it would pain me.'

She cited Rumi, 'The sea takes care of the waves till they reach the shore'. And then told Bhanu, 'Your waves of pain are being taken care of from above, Bhanu. The healing has begun. That is why you were less sad while remembering your father.'

At home, no one had an appetite for dinner, so Bhanu retired to her room with her mother. After some small talk, she told her mother about Bhushan's emails. Mother was immediately alert, 'Did you reply?'

Bhanu said, 'To the first email, yes; just a single-lined, impersonal, courteous reply. I thought that not replying would seem callous.'

'And the other one?'

'I deleted it without opening it.'

Mother thought about it for a while, and then asked, 'Bhanu, are you sure you don't want to read it? It seems to me that you have overcome Zanskar enough to read his email dispassionately. Who knows, he might just have wanted to share his grief or tell you something he could not tell anyone else. Remember Buddy's words; if you are able to help somebody, it's your privilege. You have shunned him, but apparently, he still depends on you.'

Bhanu replied, 'Maa, firstly, I am not completely over Zanskar. True, I have moved on, but it is a deep wound. It still hurts at times. But even if you are right, I can sense his motive behind writing to me. Under the guise of sharing his grief, he wants pardon and acceptance.'

Mother, 'Don't presume, Bhanu. I would suggest you retrieve the email and read it.'

Bhanu could not help marvelling at her mother's sense of fairness. Even after knowing everything, she wanted her to give him a fair hearing! Aloud, though, she faked annoyance, 'Maa! Whose side are you on?'

'It's not about taking sides, Bhanu. It's about not missing a chance to be helpful to someone if and when you are able to. That's our biggest learning from Buddy. And after all, reading is not replying. You always have the option not to reply if you're not comfortable with what he had to say. My opinion is that you should hear him out.'

Bhanu pondered; her mother had a point.

'Okay, I will read the email, but the deal is, I reserve my right not to reply.'

'Of course.'

Her mother went to the kitchen as Bhanu retrieved the email from the bin. Bhushan had not used any possessive noun before her name. Oddly, that put her off. A fleeting wish passed across her mind as she began to read, *can't he have said, 'Dear Bhanu' instead of just, 'Bhanu'?*

Bhanu,

Thank you for the condolence message.

I don't know whether I have the right to write to you or not. I don't even know whether you will read this or not. I only know that I have to write to you, or else I will become emotionally dysfunctional. The overpowering aloneness is smothering me even amidst so many well-meaning people—my family, friends and well-wishers, they all want to reach out to me, but it's as if I don't want to come out of the void. I have become uncommunicative. Hand on my heart, there is only one person who can bring me back from the edge. That is you, and that is why I am writing to you. Even if you don't read it, I would have told you, which is enough to make me feel better.

My father is no more. I am suddenly the head of the family and the business, and that has changed my priorities overnight. New responsibilities, new roles… it's surprising how a sudden tragedy changes a person's life.

However, I am not writing to talk about those matters. I know that I will ultimately cope. What I won't be able to cope with is spending the rest of my life with a woman with whom I don't bond at all. And after having loved someone else the way I did, it is all the more difficult to make room for Brinda in my life. I know this is grossly unfair to her, but then, love has seldom been a fair game. Will it not be all the more unfair if I accept her now and then make every day of her life miserable after marriage? I will see you in Brinda every time I make love to her, her voice will sound like yours whenever she calls. My marriage with Brinda is doomed to be a loveless affair, shackling both of us to a lifetime of misery.

I have reached a decision, Bhanu, and I am writing to convey it. I will talk it out with Brinda and convince her that it is in everybody's interest to end this alliance of convenience in which she has been cajoled. It may devastate her, but that will be temporary. She will ultimately realize that separation was a lesser evil and get over it.

I will persuade her that both she and I deserve a better life.

After Brinda and I have parted ways, will you still be around, Bhanu?

Bhushan.'

Bhanu was okay until she read the last line. Then her insides erupted, *How dare he!*

She started typing a furious reply, 'NO. You have lost the plot. You are doing this to get me back, but grow up, that's NOT gonna happen—ever. It hasn't been easy for me so far, don't make it worse by making it look like I am a homewrecker.'

Just then, mother entered the room. Bhanu took out her anger on her, 'Mum, why did you push me into reading his email? Didn't I tell you he will end up trying to win me back?'

'I had also said that you reserve the right not to reply.'

Bhanu shot back, 'Can you give me the right to un-read it instead?

Then she broke down. Bhushan's email had rattled her. The strong and self-assured Bhanu was determined not to be swayed by his peptalk, yet her softer, vulnerable side felt like giving in; he was her first love after all. Like a pendulum, her heart was swinging wildly between the extremes of love and loathing. On top of it, the homewrecker tag!

Mother understood, and waited patiently for her storm to calm.

When Bhanu spoke, her voice was a cracking whisper, 'Maa, now that I've read the email, I have to reply. Else, I might be labelled as a homewrecker, and that's something I will never be able to reconcile with."

Mother nodded her agreement. Bhanu showed her Bhushan's

email, and also her unsent reply.

Mother reasoned with Bhanu, 'Well, it's clear he would have never been able to accept Brinda, with or without you in his life. So, you are not a homewrecker; stop feeling guilty. I do agree that a reply is necessary, but don't be abrasive, Bhanu. Your father has taught you to be humble even in rejection.'

Seeing her mother's point, Bhanu re-drafted her reply.

> It's your life and your decision, sir. I have nothing to do with either of them anymore. I hope this answers your query in the last line. Good luck. Have a good life.
>
> P.S.: Whatever you do, don't ever let the homewrecker muck be thrown at me. You owe that much to me.

Bhanu sent the email and hugged her mother.

9

Separation Is the Lesser Evil

At times, we don't respect people's wish to withdraw from our lives. We keep clinging to them in hope until they close the door on us. Then we sulk at the rejection!

Bhanu's directness in the email made Bhushan realize with finality that he had lost her. He blamed his mother for it and broached the subject one evening after dinner, 'Mummy, you know very well that I never wanted to get engaged with Brinda, but you forced your choice on me. You wrongly presumed that you knew who and what was best for me. My generation's perceptions on marriage have changed since your time, Mummy. We take marriage more personally than your generation used to. Brinda and I are simply not compatible with each other. We may make a nice couple in photographs, but that's it. There is no deeper connection between us. I told you so repeatedly, yet you kept on pursuing the alliance unmindfully. It is as if you wanted an ideal, obedient bahu for yourself more than a suitable wife for me. It is a good alliance where everything fits perfectly except the couple.'

Bhushan's mother downplayed it and said, 'This is just your infatuation, son. You will realize in time that Brinda is an ideal match for you. Looks-wise also, she looks so much like that famous star Rasmi. You need a worthy life companion, and the family needs an efficient homemaker from our known circles, especially now that your Daddy is no more…'

Bhushan was irked further by her indifference, 'Don't try to score emotional points by dragging Daddy into the matter. And I have realized in Zanskar what type of a girl I want…'

That made his mother sit up, 'Why? Don't tell me something happened during your trek!'

Bhushan replied, 'Something did happen, Mummy. I met my match there. She was a fellow trekker from Mumbai. Her name is Bhanu. Our portrait would not have been as nice as that of Brinda and mine, but we bonded perfectly, as if we were made for each other. We fell madly in love and committed to each other too.'

Mother was aghast. Her worst fears were coming true. She looked at Bhushan unbelievingly, 'NO! But you are engaged to Brinda! How could you…'

Bhushan interrupted, 'How could I? True, how could I bond with a girl of my choice when you have tied me down with one of your choices? But relax, Mummy, it's over now.'

Mother was anxious; she wanted the entire story, 'Bhushan, tell me honestly. What happened in Zanskar?'

And so Bhushan told her, 'I had not told Bhanu about Brinda. I had thought I would tell her after the relationship had matured. Honestly, though, I guess it was the fear of losing her that was holding me back from telling her. Meanwhile, she overheard my talk with Brinda when Dad suffered the stroke, and it was all over within fifteen minutes.'

Bhushan also told her about their face-off in Delhi and then wrapped it up, 'I emailed Bhanu twice last week. The first email was to inform her about Daddy's demise. In the second email, I told her about my decision to end the engagement with Brinda…'

'What???' Mother sprang up from the sofa. Her disbelief and anger were quite visible, 'You decided to break your engagement? Why? And with whose permission?'

Bhushan expected that outburst. He kept his voice calm but firm, 'Mummy, sit down. Accept the inevitable. I will not be able to be a good husband to Brinda. This engagement should have never happened in the first place. Better to end it before it ruins two lives. Brinda is very a beautiful look-alike of a Bollywood star, perfectly groomed, an ideal homemaker, one of the most eligible brides for a section of our society, but unfortunately, I don't belong there. She deserves better, a happy marriage, which I will never be able to give her. I will talk it out with her one of these days and free her from this bondage.'

By then, his mother was hysterical, 'You have gone mad, Bhushan! You won't get a match like Brinda in our entire community. Do you know that her family gets proposals for her even now? She is a perfect combination of beauty and cultured upbringing. She had won the Miss Beautiful Face pageant twice in her college. She looks so much like that famous Rasmi, — exactly like her twin sister. The boys in her college used to call her 'Dream Girl'. It is a pride and privilege to have her as part of our family. And you—you want to reject her?! I won't let that happen. I know who is behind this. It's that cunning woman. I am sure she has got some black magic done on you.and blinded you.' Then she looked up at the ceiling and complained, 'Oh God, no, first you snatched away my husband from me, and now my son too…'

Bhushan lost his cool at his mother's less-than-decent

reference to Bhanu, 'Mummy! Don't judge someone you have not even met. Do you know her reply to my second email? She has firmly rejected any chance of a reunion with a plea, "Whatever you do, don't ever let the homewrecker muck be thrown at me. You owe that much to me." Mummy, Bhanu is different. I still remember what she had told me in Zanskar when she walked away from me—"I would like to win my man, not steal him from someone."'

Bhushan's mother gave him a shrewd, knowing smile, as if to say, 'I know her type too well to fall for their make-believe morality.'

A disgusted Bhushan threw up his hands, 'Mummy, it's beyond you to understand someone like Bhanu. Just know that she has nothing to do with my decision to break my engagement. I would have ended it even if I had never met Bhanu.'

He ended with a warning, 'Don't ever bring Bhanu in this mess again.'

Bhushan's mother was hurt and enraged at what she thought was a threat from Bhushan. She fumed, 'Look who is answering back! My only son, my flesh and blood! Where was your Bhanu when your mother sold off her ornaments to pay for your tuition? Who slept on an empty stomach to make sure that you did not? And today, you take the side of that ...'

She muttered, 'Bitch' between sobs, and then her voice trailed off.

Bhushan was past the tipping point. Blinded by rage, not knowing how to respond to his mother's unthinkable utterance, he walked out of the room, banging the door behind him. With the door dividing them, he shouted at his mother, 'Mummy, enough! I have a mind and a life of my own, and I can judge what is right for me. *Stop* meddling in my affairs from now. My decision is final. Consider my engagement with Brinda broken. And for the last time, don't bring Bhanu into this ever again.'

Bhushan walked away, stamping his feet. On the other side of the door, his mother slumped to the floor, feeling utterly helpless.

The next morning, Bhushan went to his mother and apologized for the showdown. She let go of her disappointment and took him in her arms. Bhushan said, 'Mummy, I don't know what overcame me.'

His mother hugged him tighter, 'Don't worry, beta. I should have realized what you have been going through. I am sorry too. But think again with a cool mind before taking the extreme step. Brinda is good for you. Mother knows best.'

Mother's misplaced confidence irked Bhushan. *She is at it again*, he thought and eased himself from his mother's embrace without saying anything.

Mother mistook Bhushan's silence as his acceptance of her wisdom. Encouraged, she went on, 'You mark my words, Bhushan. You will soon overcome your infatuation for Bhanu and will realize how right I was in selecting Brinda for you.'

Bhushan gave up on his mother and told himself, *She will never understand me; worse, she does not want to understand me, so what's the point in arguing with her? I will simply go ahead and do what I want to.*

This is how generational gaps are created. One more family fell prey to it that day. In those few moments, something snapped between Bhushan and his mother. The damage was done.

During the next few days, Bhushan immersed himself in his work like a possessed man.

Brinda made it a point to call Bhushan once a day. Being of caring nature, she would fuss over him. Bhushan disliked such overtures while at work, and the fact that they came from Brinda made them even more annoying. He kept his replies curt. At times, he told her that he was busy and ended the call. When this became a pattern, Brinda thought it was better to clear the matter. She said one day, 'Listen, Bhush, I call because I care. I can understand your state of mind and want to be there for you, but it's almost like I'm smothering you…'

Bhushan was edgy, 'Don't you realize I am at work? Your badgering can wait.'

Brinda was hurt, 'Badgering? That's harsh, Bhush?'

And Bhushan was gross, 'Oh, women!'

The way he said it hit Brinda hard, 'Bhush! *Stop it*, or else…'

'Or else what, huh?' he challenged her and hung up.

When he was free in the evening, Bhushan thought about the spat with Brinda.

It's my fault, he admitted. *Why am I putting off the inevitable? The more I dilly-dally, the worse it is going to get.* And he made up his mind, *this has to end as soon as possible.*

He called Brinda. She was genuinely surprised.

'Wow! You actually called! Want to say sorry, no?'

Bhushan just said, 'Brinda, we need to talk. I will pick you up at six.'

She was overjoyed, 'I'll be ready at six.'

~

Bhushan took the Mathura Highway and drove until they approached an eatery. He had resolved to handle that evening's talk in the least damaging manner and thought a compliment would be a good way to begin, 'Looking pretty, Karisma.'

Brinda did look stunning. Unsuspecting of what lay ahead, she beamed; it was the first time Bhushan had complimented her. His praise produced sudden desire in her. So, when he asked her if she wanted something to eat or drink, she replied, 'I am both hungry and thirsty.'

However, Bhushan pretended not to have noticed the lust in her eyes and began, 'Brinda, I really appreciate the way you have shouldered responsibilities in my home in the last fortnight after Dad's demise. It was not expected of you yet, but you volunteered. Emotionally too, you have been a great succour to the family.'

It was Brinda's day of surprises. Still beaming, she patted his hand and said, 'Papaji was my father too, Bhush. I miss him as much as you do.'

Bhushan uttered a meek 'thank you' in reply.

By then, Brinda had realized that Bhushan was in no mood for romance, so she checked herself and listened to him, 'Brinda, you are a beautiful young lady with charm and grace, but more so, you are a wonderful person. With your immaculate upbringing, I am sure you would make a dream homemaker.'

There was no let-up in Brinda's surprises, 'Wow, Bhush, I am flattered. You made my evening, really.'

'I am glad I did, Brinda. However, I have an unpleasant matter that I want to talk about. I know it will hurt you, and I apologize in advance, but it must be brought up without further delay.'

Brinda was perplexed, this was not the script for the evening, but aloud, she asked him, 'What's the matter, Bhush? You look as if you are far away from here.'

'In fact, I am. I admit I am existing at two levels.'

'You miss Papaji badly, isn't it? I can understand.'

'I do, but it's not about Dad, Brinda.'

'Then what is it? Tell me, I can't stand the suspense.'

Bhushan took a deep breath. He tried to calm his nerves and gather the courage to say what he had to say. He was determined to sound as less hurting as possible. He chose his words carefully, 'Brinda, I met someone during the Zanskar trek. Her name is Bhanu.'

And Brinda's demeanour collapsed like a house of cards. She shrunk in the seat, looking disbelievingly at Bhushan. Her voice sounded hollow, 'What do you mean?'

'You know what I mean.'

Brinda sat motionless and silent. Her sheltered upbringing had not readied her to handle such a sudden, unforeseen personal crisis all by herself; she always had someone to take care of her problems. She sat very still. Bhushan waited out those moments. After what seemed like an eternity, she managed to find her voice, 'No, Bhush, you can't do this to me. Please don't do this to me. We are engaged. We're going to get married soon.'

Although Bhushan had prepared for the moment, he was crushed by guilt. He said, 'Brinda, I can well understand how hurt and wrong you must feel. Believe me, I had no intention of betraying you. It just happened.'

Brinda's face cringed in painful surprise, 'It just happened? How could you let it happen, Bhush? An engagement is a commitment; don't you have any sense of accountability towards me? What if I had let that happen to me and then said, it just happened?'

Bhushan replied too quickly, 'I would walk out of the alliance.'

That was harsh, but Brinda tried to reason with him, 'Listen, Bhush, there are rich, handsome and eligible boys who pursue me even today. On Facebook, I get mistaken for Rasmi and I'm flooded with greetings on her birthday. Without indulging in vanity, I am much sought-after even today. But I am a one-man woman. It's not in my nature to succumb to temptations once I am committed.'

Brinda paused to throw more weight behind her words. It was now or never for her. She pleaded, 'Bhush, we have to make it work. In my heart, I am already married to you. You can't just walk out on me.'

Then she started folding her hands, but Bhushan stopped her, 'No Brinda, don't ever do that to anyone—anyone—if you are not in the wrong, and in our case, you are on the right side. It is I who should be folding my hands in front of you. I should have remained firm when I was being cajoled into our engagement. I now realize what great harm a man brings upon an innocent woman when he is weak and indecisive—when he lets himself get dragged into a matrimonial alliance against his will.'

Then he added gently, 'You deserve better, Brinda, I mean it. We both have loved wholeheartedly, but unfortunately, not each other. And having loved so, both of us know that we cannot love anyone else like that. For me, a marriage without love is a trap, a sham. Trust me, I tried very hard to reconcile to reality, but I have failed. I take total blame for this. People will gossip for a while and then move on. You, too, will get over it once the initial shock has subsided. I have thought very deeply; an early separation is in everybody's favour. Breaking an engagement is a lesser evil than a divorce.'

As Bhushan's words sank in, she asked, 'You won't rethink?'

He did not reply.

The hurt, wronged woman in Brinda then raised her head, 'Bhanu, may I know what she has that I don't?'

Bhushan tried to stop her, 'Look, Brinda, let's not get into that...' but her wound had already ruptured. She leaned toward Bhushan and demanded, 'Why not? I deserve to know where she scores over me.'

Bhushan shot her a cautionary glance, 'Don't bring Bhanu into this Brinda. She has nothing to do with this.'

Controlling himself immediately, Bhushan explained, 'It was very brief. Bhanu did not know I was engaged to you. As fate would have it, she overheard our conversation on the satellite phone and walked out of my life. The last thing she wants is to be a homewrecker. So keep her out of this.'

'So you're telling me it's over between you two, and yet you want us to separate? Why? This is ridiculous! Why, Bhush? Why are you doing this?'

Rather than answering her directly, Bhushan said, 'Believe me, Brinda, I have thought about it long and hard. I am being fair to you.'

'No, I don't believe you,' Brinda shot back, 'I don't buy that. You are just trying to be nice while making way for that bitch.'

'Brinda! *No!*' Bhushan shouted at her, as he had shouted at his mother.

Brinda, too, was agitated, 'Don't give me that crap, Bhush. I know enough about such scheming women.'

Then it came out of her mouth involuntarily, 'Bitch.'

And Bhushan exploded,'Enough! It's you who is sounding like a bitch right now.'

Brinda had never been called names. She looked disbelievingly at Bhushan, and her face grimaced in pain. Clasping both her hands on her mouth, she barely managed to contain her cry of outrage. She felt her breath was failing her, and in two minutes, she passed out.

Bhushan sprang up, sprinkled water on Brinda's face, kept on calling her name loudly, and mildly pinched her face to check her reflexes. Brinda responded to him after a few minutes and opened her eyes. Relieved, Bhushan said, 'Are you okay, Brinda? I am sorry, Brinda, I truly am. I don't know what blind rage overtook my senses.'

Brinda just said, 'Take me home.'

Bhushan asked again, 'Are you okay? Do you want to rest for some time? Perhaps a cold drink?'

'No, just take me home.'

There was no more conversation between them until Bhushan entered the city and took the turn to her home.

When they reached Brinda's home, he said, 'Wait, I will open the door for you.'

'No, I am fine,' she said and walked away from Bhushan.

Bhushan shook his head in dejection.

~

The next evening, the two families met at Brinda's home. Brinda looked haggard and seemed to have lost weight overnight. Her eyes were swollen, but otherwise, her face was composed and solemn and reflected the resolve of a person who would not take injustice and pain anymore. After mandatory pleasantries and the motions of snacks and refreshments, Bhushan's mother started to set a context to the meeting, 'Kanayyalalji and Urvashiji, we have been friends for more than a decade, our ties are respected in our community. We have shared our joys and sorrows. Our families know each other so well, which is why we thought this was a good alliance. But perhaps destiny has other plans. I tried hard to convince Bhushan but...'

Brinda interrupted in a firm yet courteous tone, taking the

matter in her hands, 'Sorry, Auntyji, this is not Bhushan's fault. We had a long chat yesterday and have mutually decided to call off our engagement. It is simple; we are not made for each other. Please forgive us for the embarrassment and pain this will cause both families, but the decision is final.'

Bhushan started to say something, but Brinda stopped him, 'Please, Bhushan, we will remain good friends and Auntyji, whenever you need me, you can count on me. I guess this settles the matter. Only the engagement is broken, not the family ties.'

She added after a pause, 'It's not a pleasant subject to talk about, so I request you all to keep this meeting brief.'

Brinda moved to the edge of her chair as if she wanted to rise up and leave. Taking the cue, everyone stood up, and after meaningless courtesies, the meeting was over. Brinda and her parents walked their guests to the car. As Bhushan started the ignition, he said, 'Brinda, thank you.'

'Not at all,' she said.

However, her eyes followed his car until it took a turn and merged in the milieu of Delhi's evening traffic.

∽

10
New Beginnings

Once again, Bhushan sought refuge in his work.

The late Bhanu Pratap Singh had ventured into retail clothing after his failed business partnership in wholesale trade. Over the years, he had created a chain of several retail stores in Delhi and NCR. He had named them after his initials, BPS. With time, the BPS brand became synonymous with a wide range of collections for the entire family, fair prices, and a friendly shopping experience. It was very rare that a customer stepped out of a BPS store without getting what they wanted.

Bhushan had grown up watching his father build his business with his sweat and blood. Now, he made it his mission to take the BPS brand to new heights. On studying the market, he realized that his main challenge was to counter the online- and mall-shopping mania. These were irreversible trends, and so he thought, *if you can't fight them, join them.*

And so Bhushan decided to get on the bandwagon. He planned to open new stores in upmarket malls and showcase renowned international clothing and fashion labels under one roof. This would give his customers an international shopping opportunity at home, without having to go on shopping sprees to London and New York and Paris. To meet the growing demands of his customers, he would go beyond clothing and offer a vast range of accessories, grooming and personal care products. In this manner, he planned for BPS to become a preferred destination for the sharp and discerning upscale shoppers.

With this vision, Bhushan moved on to selecting a good name for the new venture. He would spend nights thinking of hundreds of names suitable for a high-street fashion and personal care store. He would mouth the options to himself even in his sleep. *Fashionistan?* He would ask himself. *Cult-Ure? Mad&Mod? Zeus? Yesss! Zeus is **the** name! It is ancient Greek yet contemporary, has an international ring to it, it's easy to mouth and remember...* Then again, he would reject Zeus and hundreds of other names. Once, he even pondered seriously on Nar-Nari. Unisex, modern yet distinctly Indian. Then he mocked his own thinking, *Nar-Nari, as in Adam-n-Eve? So kitschy.* So, that name also went for a toss.

In the end, he left it to spontaneous inspiration, which he was sure, would strike him unexpectedly.

One late night, as he was about to retire, he looked up at his father's photo on the wall. Just below the picture were his handwritten words, 'The Light Inside Me.' He smiled at BPS, 'Now you are also the fire in my belly, Mr Bhanu Pratap Singh. Bless me with a good store name.'

And it was as if his wish was granted! Inspiration came calling—*Why not name the store as Bhanu?*

Goosebumps ran through his body. *Bhanu?* He toyed with the name. *Yes, Bhanu, after your father and your first love.* And he decided on the name instantly, 'Bhanu—The Lifestyle Store'.

~

Bhushan had chosen the location for the new store in Khan Market, where the stylish, young crowd, the upwardly mobile, and the upper crust of Delhi mingled. The store was housed in a stately white building with an ornate colonial façade. It boasted of 13,000 square feet of sprawling shopping space spread across three floors. The interiors were marked by understated elegance and cosy comfort. Numerous sections of Indian and international clothing, lifestyle, and accessories' were laid out in such a way that selections could be made in an unhurried, relaxed manner. The range of merchandise in each section was truly vast and versatile. Adhering to his father's principles, the store ensured that nobody stepped out without finding what they were looking for. It had taken Bhushan close to a year of backbreaking effort to build the place according to his vision, but the sweat and toil were worth it. As he watched the store come up before his eyes each day, Bhushan felt gratified; he had been able to keep his promise of taking his father's legacy to new heights.

Before he knew it, it was the day of the launch! Nearly everyone who was invited was present at the event. Bhushan entered the packed venue and received immediate attention. He wore a charcoal-grey suit with a solid, aqua green, silk shirt and a crème-coloured broad tie. His hair was gelled and stylishly combed upwards without a parting. His 6'1" frame looked comfortably settled in a plush, burgundy leather swivel chair, oozing quiet authority and charm as he spoke briefly.

'Ladies and gentlemen, thank you for coming. We are excited to launch this new endeavour which will be home to the famed and celebrated international fashion labels in India. We are venturing into this area with a mission to appease the innate desire of contemporary Indian women and men to look their best, no matter what the occasion. I hope our efforts will place them on par with their global counterparts. It is about creating synergies between India and the world in the contexts of dressing, fashion and personal care. Although international in its ambition, our venture is Indian in its ethos, and so we've named it Bhanu—The Lifestyle Store

'Bhanu means the sun. It is a tribute to my late father, Shri Bhanu Pratap Singh, whose blessings, I am sure, will nurture this infant venture as sunrays raise a sapling. Thank you all once again, enjoy the evening.'

~

By sheer coincidence, in Mumbai, Bhanu was switching channels on that laid back evening and chanced upon the live coverage of that launch. She sat up with a start as Bhushan's tight close-up covered the screen from edge to edge. He looked straight at the cameras, at her, 'Bhanu means the sun. It is a tribute to my late father Shri Bhanu Pratap Singh...'

Bhanu missed several heartbeats. WTF! Those were her lines!

When she had recovered, she muttered, 'Clever bastard,' as she noted how he had played upon the name.

He was looking devastatingly handsome. She could not take her eyes off the TV screen.

And he looked so sorted. 'As if you have side-stepped your past. Not fair!' She murmured to herself.

Throughout the evening after the live coverage was finished and even at night, images of Bhushan's handsome face and his cool demeanour kept coming back at Bhanu. Around midnight, she thought she had had enough. She shouted at the walls, 'Go away!!!'

But Bhushan refused to go. He was all around her. She cried a bit and wondered helplessly, *Why is first love so stubborn?*

In Delhi, Bhushan put in treacherous hours and days to transform the store into the best fashion destination Delhi ever had. Within months of its launch, he had finalized franchise deals with three more leading American and two Italian fashion houses. In the accessories' segment, he focused on leather goods, footwear, eyewear and watches, and picked up the top five youthful brands in each segment for negotiations.

Next, Bhushan turned his attention to perfumes and scents, which shifted his focus to France. It was April, and Delhi was readying to face a torrid summer. Bhushan had worked tirelessly for many months without taking a single day off. The idea of mixing business with leisure in France immediately appealed to him. And what better place to unwind than the French Riviera? Bhushan ticked 15 days off his calendar for his France tour, out of which a full week would be strictly no-work, the workaholic Bhushan mandated himself.

He set his eyes on the quaint, scenic Grasse-Nice-Cannes Riviera trail.

Bhushan recalled that the Cannes Film Festival is held during the Indian summer. On a hunch, he checked the festival's dates for that year and bingo! They coincided with his vacation. Although nowhere near being a cinema connoisseur, Bhushan had an inborn liking for international films

'Cannes, here I come!' He said as he drifted off to sleep and then added a quick postscript, 'Alone.'

Little did he know that company awaited him at Cannes.

11

A Second Chance at First Love

Bhushan had set himself a hectic schedule in Paris. He had back-to-back meetings with three leading perfume manufacturers on day one. Two of them offered their entire catalogue of scented products for the franchise. This included not just their wide range of body scents but also soaps, talcum powders, gels, lotions, bath preparations, a complete line of aromatherapy products, and even scented candles! On the second day, he had lined up some more presentations. By the end of day five, Bhushan had reached advanced levels of talks and finalizations of deals with several leading French perfume brands. With such an impressive line-up, his store would be the perfume capital of India! That thought summed up his business engagement.

With work out of his way, Bhushan got footloose and explored Paris's landmarks for the next three days. At the Eiffel Tower, he spent much time on the breezy top floor. The three glasses of rose champagne served at a small bar made him pensive. It was already eight in the evening and darkness had descended on the city far below. The urban expanse was wrapped in velvety black. The moving vehicles seemed like millions of fireflies swarming the city roads. At over a thousand feet above ground level, Bhushan felt suspended from reality and drifted into a time warp where he could shuttle back and forth at will. The champagne helped. As he gulped one more mouthful, Bhanu emerged from the back of his mind, and with her, a torrent of fond, wishful affection that he had dammed for so long. Caged emotions exploded and went awry over Bhushan's tipsy head. It swirled and he went on a roller-coaster ride of uncensored, raw emotions. The fantasy trip was far better than the real experiences. Bhushan lost all sense of time until it was 9:30.

'9:30!' He exclaimed as he looked at his watch. He tossed the empty champagne container in the waste bin and headed for dinner at a popular first-floor restaurant that boasted of best views of night-time Paris. The hostess greeted him warmly and guided him to his reserved table. The interior was chic and elegant, and the subdued lighting supplemented the illumination pouring in from outside. The low, soft music was very romantic. Like all of Paris, everything about the restaurant was a celebration of love and togetherness. It depressed Bhushan. He muttered under his breath, 'Bhanu, I miss you sorely, terribly.'

～

The next morning, Bhushan hit the Riviera trail. His first stop was at Grasse, a six-something hour journey from Paris by train. His window seat gave him amazing views of the French hinterland. The landscapes changed every minute, yet they remained steadfast in their European character of resplendent, unspoilt natural splendour with minimal human interference. Bhushan thanked himself for not having taken a flight.

Once in Grasse, Bhushan was transported to another universe, one with magnificent rolling hills and endless miles of flower fields that draped the earth in myriads of purples, yellows, whites, reds, oranges, blues. The flowers offered sensuous, addictive whiffs as far as the nose could smell. Bhushan understood first-hand why Grasse was called the world's perfume capital. Standing in the middle of a lavender field, he took a deep breath and filled his lungs with the purest air he had ever inhaled. Letting it out slowly, he thought, *this place is an alchemist's wonderland.*

The next day, on his visit to Nice, Bhushan noticed a billboard at a perfumery that said, 'Create your own perfume in 2 hours.'

Bhushan was immediately intrigued. He asked his chauffer to drive into the perfumery. At the reception counter, he learned that the two-hours-long course was a DIY (Do-It-Yourself) approach to creating one's personal perfume—not only that, the formula was stored in the company's archives and given a code so that one could order a fresh supply of the perfume whenever needed. He immediately signed up for the late-noon batch.

After an introductory talk at the workshop, the perfume expert, called a 'nose,' produced several glass bottles with perfume concentrates. She then asked the participants to suggest a fragrance theme for their personal perfume. Bhushan came up with the concept of garden-fresh tuberoses with a note of meadow roses. He knew that Bhanu loved tuberoses; it involuntarily dominated his perfume theme. The 'nose' immediately approved it and added that Bhushan could even name it to create a unique signature perfume. He responded instantly. He wanted it to be called 'First Love'. The lady was impressed. She said in her elementary English, 'Tuberose smell is strong, but its petals are very delicate. And it is white in colour. So, tuberose is like first love, which is delicate but strong, pure as the white colour and also very soft. And the rose is the eternal symbol of love. That makes a perfect formula for 'First Love'. Well done, monsieur!'

Bhushan was flattered. He gave her a smug smile.

Within an hour, the first batch of the First Love perfume was ready. The lady handed Bhushan a 10 oz bottle. He took a whiff of it and let the sensation spread through his body. His every atom screamed her name. Aloud, all he could tell the lady was, 'Merci'.

She smiled in acknowledgment and asked, 'Monsieur, can I make suggestion?'

Bhushan nodded so the lady suggested, 'Monsieur, first love translates to *premier amour* in French. It sounds more stylish as a French perfume name. You approve?'

Bhushan liked the ring to it. It was chic, simple and honest. He thanked her again, 'Merci!' and added, 'It sounds great!'

And the lady beamed at Bhushan.

That's how, First Love was reborn as *Premier Amour*.

~

Bhushan spent two days in Nice and then reached Cannes. The city was already in the grips of festival fever. The floating population of visitors gave it a wonderful multicultural air. People from different nationalities were not characterized by their language alone; their body language, attitude, attire, pitch and tone of conversation, and even their hand and face gestures formed a pattern of communication. Solemn-faced young girls with slightly rigid strides were most likely a ballet group from Russia. In contrast, a crew of filmmakers from the US, dressed in oversized, loud Hawaiian shirts, had a carefree, fun disposition. After a few hours on the streets, Bhushan devised a guessing game for himself—observing a group from a distance, he would decide its nationality, then approach them for a brief introduction, and determine whether his guess was right or not. By evening, Bhushan had done seventeen rounds of the game and won thirteen of them. In the process, he began to understand how cinema was perceived and made differently in various parts of the world.

The next morning, while talking to the friendly receptionist at the hotel where he had put up, Bhushan learned that there was an Indian group staying in the same hotel. When on foreign soil, coming across countrymen always creates instant interest in them. Bhushan inquired who they were. The receptionist said that their short film had won the third prize in Cinéfondation, the competitive platform for short and medium-length films at Cannes. They were here to receive the award. Impressed, Bhushan checked if they were at the hotel then, but the receptionist replied that they had gone for press interviews at the India Centre. So he left a short message along with his business card for the director, Satish Mandal.

Dear Mr Mandal,

Greetings from a fellow Indian, and congratulations on this remarkable feat. It makes India proud. I have put up in the same hotel—will be honoured to meet you over drinks.

Cheers,
Bhushan 'B.P.' Singh

12
The Stage Is Set for the Reunion

When the team returned, the director read the note. The interviews had gone very well, so he was in a cheerful mood. He passed the note to Bhanu, who was just two steps behind him, and joked, 'Somebody has come all the way from India to buy us drinks!'

Bhanu laughed, 'Never say no to free booze'.

She had earned her Cannes visit by sheer hard work and a bit of luck, and wanted to make the most of it. For her post-graduation thesis in Mass Communication, Bhanu had chosen the subject, 'Documentary Films—An Effective Means to Address Social Issues in India.' Coincidentally, Suresh Mandal had been making a film that was perfect as a case study for Bhanu's thesis. When she approached Suresh, he had suggested that she join the filming for a fortnight to understand the social issue in its real-life context. Bhanu had jumped at the opportunity and hit the ground running. Once she was a part of the team, she was consumed by the passion and commitment of everyone who worked with Suresh. She felt that she *had* to play a more active role in the project. Looking at her excellent English, Suresh had asked her to do the subtitles. They hit it off so well that soon, she became his defacto assistant. So, when the film made it to Cannes, Satish asked Bhanu to join the team to receive the award. From the small town of Gangtok to the metropolis that is Mumbai, to Cannes, the haven of cinematic pursuits, Bhanu's life had taken her to bigger and better places. And if somebody was offering free booze, it was more than welcome!

'Here,' Satish said, and handed her the note. She read it, then read the name, and then went numb. Her first reaction was disbelief. Him? Here? Impossible. She checked the attached business card. Not only the name but the logo of his store confirmed that it was him. She felt as if she was made of wax, or that mercury was flowing in her blood. But even in that state of shock, one thought surfaced in her mind.

He has finally caught up with me. He is here, in the same hotel, in flesh and blood. He has asked to meet us. There is no way I can wish him away. How will I face him?

Satish called out to her, 'What happened? Come on.'

Bhanu had to make a tremendous effort to sound normal, 'Nothing, you guys go ahead. I'll join you in a minute.'

She found a vacant seat in the lounge and threw herself in it. Slumped, she read the note again. Her face flushed and her eyes reddened as warm tears started welling up. She knew she wouldn't be able to hold them for long. She rushed to the restroom and let go of self-control. A torrent of unruly emotions gushed out.

Why was her past trying to trespass on her present?

Why was providence giving him a chance to make a comeback in her life?

And she too, why was she unable to hate him as completely as before?

Why did it feel like she was touching him when she touched the name on his business card?

Why was first love so stubborn?

Part 3

Rising in Love

13

A Face-Off That Changes Everything

'I am in the group that you have asked to meet with. Satish has asked me to convey to you that we can meet tomorrow evening. Talk to me on this number before that. And please, no drama in public.' Bhanu scribbled her number hurriedly on the note and left it for Bhushan at the reception before joining her group.

Bhushan was jolted when he read the note in the evening. He lost his balance for a few seconds. The receptionist asked with concern, 'Are you okay, monsieur?'

He nodded, 'Yes I am fine, just a drink or two too many.'

He barely managed to thank her and rushed to his room. As he crashed on the bed, his thoughts went awry.

Bhanu! Of all the places on the earth, here, in Cannes!

How come?

Why had destiny brought her here at this time?

Why was fate making their face-off inevitable?

Why was he so panic-stricken, gutless, at the thought of meeting her again?

Why did he want to take two steps at a time to reach the fifth floor, crash into Bhanu's room and take her in his arms?

Why was first love so stubborn?

~

'Hello?' Bhushan's voice trembled a bit when he called Bhanu.

She took the call but could not speak.

He sounded unsure, tentative, 'Hi, you had asked me to call.'

After a few seconds, she managed to find her voice and spoke at a stretch, 'Look, I just want to tell you that I am here in a professional capacity. There should be no drama in public when we face each other. In fact, it is best that we pretend to be strangers. Can you pull it off?'

Bhushan said, 'You are asking for too much, but I will try. Can we not feign acquaintance as Zanskar co-trekkers?'

Bhanu replied, 'Ok,' and was about to end the call when Bhushan said, 'Bhanu, I badly want to talk to you for a few minutes. Papa is no more, and…'

'Look, even I have lost my Paa, but that doesn't mean…' and she realized she had bungled.

'Whatttttt?' When? How? Why didn't you tell me?' Bhushan was shocked.

'It is no longer necessary for you to know what happens in my life.'

Her bluntness took him off guard, 'Have we become enemies?'

'Not even that. We simply don't know each other. I asked you to call just to forewarn you that there should be no drama.'

Bhushan started to say something, but Bhanu cut him off, 'Look, we have nothing else to talk about. Just don't embarrass me when we meet.'

She got his WhatsApp message ten minutes later, 'Need to talk, for just a few minutes. Don't ignore.'

But she did just that. Another ten minutes, another message, 'Just a few mins, Armani Caffé, La Croisette promenade, in one hour?'

Bhanu quickly typed a curt reply, 'NO. Stop.'

Bhushan texted back even faster, 'Pls. Once. For a few mins. I won't bring up anything from the past.'

The texting was being noticed by others and was becoming conspicuous. Bhanu was sure Bhushan wouldn't give up, so she typed back, 'K'.

Immediately, she regretted her decision; *why did I let him talk me into this?*

~

Bhushan was already at the café when Bhanu entered. The long stretch of the sea-facing boulevard wore a festive look. It seemed as if the entire town had poured out there.

Bhushan got up from his chair, an awkward half-smile on his face, as she walked toward him.

Observing her from a distance, he murmured, 'She looks more elegant and taller than ever.'

Bhanu, on the other end, thought, *He looks older than 24.*

Bhushan, observing her dress, *Looks smart in the abstract chiffon one-piece, and the breezy blue stole. So French.*

Bhanu thought back, as if in reply, *And whatever happened to his boyish charm and dirty jeans? This typical three-piece suit and all, he looks boring.*

She is more of a lady now, with that poise and confidence

Success has ruined his sex appeal, argh, which girl will fall for this couch-potato-in-the-making?

Gawd, she's inviting glances!

I just hope he doesn't offer a hand-shake, mine are already sweaty.

He did not extend his hand when she reached his table. He did not do anything. He just stood there transfixed for a few moments. The attendant drew the chair for Bhanu and said, 'Mademoiselle.'

Bhushan regained his manner and smiled at Bhanu, 'Hi.'

She smiled back with a polite 'hi' as she settled in her chair. Opening the conversation with an impersonal line, she said, 'Compliments on the success of your lifestyle store. I noticed it on your business card.'

'Thank you, and thank you for coming.' He said and asked, 'So, what brings you to Cannes?'

She told him, and then asked him back, 'And what brings you here?'

'I am expanding my lifestyle business and including the full range of body, bath and atmospheric scents to our product line. When it comes to fragrances, where else to come than to France?'

'True,' Bhanu agreed.

Comfort was building between the two. Bhushan started telling Bhanu more about the store, beginning from the day of its launch. Bhanu managed to keep a straight face, not giving him any clue that she had constantly been following the store's progress ever since its launch.

When he had finished, she asked, 'Hmmm, nice. But why that name for your store? It's old-fashioned for a lifestyle store.'

'It's a tribute to my late father, whose name, as you know, begins with Bhanu.' Then, the explanation, 'Also, Bhanu means "the sun", so I hope Dad's blessings keep nurturing the store like sunrays.'

He's copied and pasted from his launch speech, Bhanu smiled inwardly.

The attendant approached to take their order. Bhanu ordered

a basil iced tea and Bhushan asked for a vanilla mocha.

As the attendant retreated, Bhanu came to the point, 'So? What did you want to talk about?'

'Why didn't you tell me about your father's tragic demise?'

'You called me here to ask that?' That was too direct, so Bhanu quickly followed it through with a polite rejoinder, 'It was such a shock, the worst days of my life. Apparently, there was no antidote to my grief. Even if I had told you, your emails wouldn't have provided me any comfort whatsoever.'

'Forget emails. I would have come down personally.'

'I know, and that is another reason why I didn't tell you. It would have given you a reason to approach me, and I did not want that.'

'You still hate me.'

Bhanu did not reply.

The attendant brought their order and left.

Bhushan said, 'Anyway, my belated condolences. I know how difficult it is to cope without a father. When did it happen?'

She told him when, and he exclaimed immediately, 'Hey wait, that's the same day my Daddy passed away!'

And Bhanu said, 'That's the third reason why I didn't tell you. I knew you were in equal pain. I wanted us to cope with our grief individually, separately. Besides, I had Mum and Buddy, my best friend, by my side. Somehow, I managed to survive the tragedy.'

'Well...' Bhushan shrugged and then asked, 'How did it happen?'

'Major heart attack in the middle of coronary bypass surgery. It got worse because he was a chronic diabetic. Doctors tried their best to retrieve his pulse, but he had already gone too far on the other side.'

Bhanu's gaze was fixed on the ice cubes in her drink. They clinked as she shook the glass vigorously. A shadow of sadness covered her face. Bhushan tried to reach out to her, but she stiffened a bit and withdrew her hands from the table. Bhushan sat there silently until the moment had passed and then told her about his father's demise, 'My father never recovered fully after the massive stroke. He kept on drifting in and out of consciousness. Then his vital organs started malfunctioning. We had been cautioned that his end was near, so it was expected. But still, it is very different when it finally happens. I felt Dad's loss the most when I lit his pyre. As his mortal remains got consumed by the raging flames, it struck me, now all I have are his photographs.'

'I know the feeling, my heartfelt sympathies.'

Bhushan nodded in acknowledgment and again tried to reach out to Bhanu. This time, she let him hold her hands after feeble resistance. They were damp and a bit cold. As he held them, they felt like they would melt, give in to his warm, comforting hold.

Just then, her phone rang. It was Satish. She quickly withdrew her hands from Bhushan's grasp, 'Hi! Boss, what's up?'

Satish said, 'Your time is what's up, girlie. Report immediately.'

Bhanu chuckled and then checked the time. She jumped, 'Gosh, I didn't realize it's 10:30! I lost track of time catching up with this long-lost friend!'

'I know how it is, Bhanu. Should we wait for you for the night-out or do you have other plans?'

Bhanu, 'Yes, of course. I mean, no, of course, not. Be there in 15.'

'Come fast, then. We're waiting.'

The call jolted Bhanu. Reality check, she told herself, what am I doing here holding hands with the guy I had vowed never to see again?

She did not bother to finish her drink. She said unceremoniously, 'I have to leave.'

'Can't you avoid it?'

'What for? To let you entice me?'

'God no, just to talk.'

She was exasperated, 'Look, it's not going to work. I won't let it work. I never wanted to meet you, but you drew me into it. Now please, I want to leave, and don't call me again.'

Bhanu got up and started walking briskly toward the exit. Bhushan went after her, quickly leaving some money on the table, 'Hey Bhanu, listen, just a sec, I have something for you,' and he began to bring out the bottle of *Premier Amour* from his coat pocket.

'No,' she said coldly and hurried to the exit.

Bhushan caught up with her, 'Let's at least walk down to the hotel together.'

'No, I need time to myself,' and he retreated.

~

Bhushan avoided going back to the hotel and hung around the boulevard until midnight. He got into a disco bar, ordered a large drink, and blankly stared at the vivacious, cheerful couples dancing their heart out on the floor. He just wanted to kill time until he was either drunk or sleepy. An attractive but garishly-dressed woman sat down beside him. Flashing a bright smile, she asked him, 'Alone? Won't you buy a lady a drink?'

Her heavy makeup made it impossible to gauge her age, but she possessed the practiced charm to catch the attention of a lonely man looking for fun. Bhushan could sniff the strong smell of her cheap perfume. He remained silent but the woman mistook it for dilemma, and pushed it further, 'What you say, mister? A few drinks and just some fun afterwards?'

Bhushan exploded, 'No, Go!'

The lady was taken aback. It was Cannes, and it was Festival time. She did not think she had done anything unreasonable to displease that man. Annoyed, she scoffed at him, 'Prick,' and walked away.

Bhushan left his drink unfinished and walked out of the bar.

The night had become chilly, and Bhushan was tipsy. He felt Bhanu's hand in his. Her soft, delicate, shapely hand was trying to fit into his firm, square palm. Her fingers were interlocked with his and holding his hand firmly. Hand in hand, they walked silently to the hotel. Still in a daze, Bhushan collected his key card, went to his room, and crashed out, still fully dressed.

~

The next day was the Awards day. Satish had invited Bhushan to attend the event as his personal guest. By six in the evening, he was ready. Dressed in a thick grey polo-neck tee and a black suit, he looked every bit like a regular at Cannes.

As he greeted Satish in the lounge, he said, 'You are all over the newspapers!'

Satish made light of his compliment, 'Flukes do happen. We did our job, gave it our best shot, and it turned out to be a winning short!'

Bhushan liked his humour, 'So that's the long and short of it?!'

Bhushan then turned to Bhanu, 'It was such a pleasure catching up yesterday.'

Bhanu was relieved. He looked calm and confident. He wasn't going to goof up after all. She joked, 'Yeah, it really seemed like ages, like, the last we met was in 1859?'

Satish introduced the group to Bhushan, and soon, he became one of them. After some casual conversation, he asked Satish, 'So what's the plan after the awards ceremony?'

'I thought you were going to knock us out with your liquid generosity?'

'I stand by my word.'

And Bhanu chipped in, 'Never say no to free booze.'

When Satish was called on the stage to receive the award, he beckoned the entire team to join him on the dais. He looked smart in his sharp lapelled black jacket and jelled hair combed back. His unkempt salt-n-pepper beard added a dash of intellect to his looks. Accepting the award, he said in a brief speech, 'This one's for India, its people, and my hardworking team. I deserve it the least.' He paused to think, 'In the socio-cultural context, India is a continent. With 22 languages and over 1600 mother-tongues, the cultural landscape is vastly diverse. Obviously, there will be cultural issues. This film is an honest attempt to bridge those cracks before they become gaps. Special thanks to Miss Bhanu Bhutia, whose analyses and insights got this film its candid character.'

Satish bowed slightly to Bhanu, who was standing beside him, and she reciprocated. The audience applauded, and Bhushan's heart burst with pride. She was dressed in a flowing black chiffon gown with ethnic mirror-work that shimmered in the limelight. A white Cinderella bow was stitched to its closed, collared neck. Her hair was tied back neatly, helping her capitalize on her broad forehead. When she smiled at the audience in acknowledgment of the ovation, Bhushan told himself, 'I would die for her.'

The team of serious filmmakers transformed into a rowdy mob as soon as they reached the hotel. Sporadic celebrations broke out. Satish uncorked the champagne bottle and sprayed it on his team in soccer match-style. There were throaty hoots and shrill jeers. Backslapping and belly poking was followed by repeated 'wwoohhooos'. A semblance of normalcy returned only after about an hour. Then Satish announced, 'Now for some official boozing!'

Graphic t-shirts and distressed jeans quickly replaced the formal Cannes attire. The mob went on a rampage at a youthful resto-bar that had an excellent menu. The first round was, of course, champagne. Bhushan raised a toast for Satish, 'To your success, Satish! And to cupboards full of awards!'

Bhanu quickly added, 'And to many more free drinks. Guys, do justice to the liquid food.'

Glasses clinked and a chorus of 'cheersss' erupted.

Satish said, 'Hic hic hurrayyy!' and the party was on.

It was obvious that both Bhanu and Bhushan had left the previous evening behind them. They just wanted to live the moment.

Once sufficiently tipsy, Bhanu came up with a weird idea, 'Hello hello attention please, let's do a DIY cocktail. Sour cherry syrup mixed with pink champagne in a 1:1 ratio. Orange pulp at the base of the glass and crushed ice floating on top.'

Nobody had heard anything like that before. The only other girl in the team made a face and said, 'Yuk no, I'm out.'

Someone differed with her, 'Sounds so much fun, let's try it, guys.'

Satish seconded the idea, 'There's a first time for everything.'

Bhushan slurred, 'Friends, life is either a risskk or nothing. Let's do it.'

So they ordered sour cherry syrup, orange pulp, and crushed ice—champagne they already had in abundance—and managed to DIY the crazy cocktail. Everybody survived the misadventure.

Bhushan complimented Bhanu, 'You are a genius when half-drunk.'

She patted her own back, 'I'm even better when fullllly drunk.'

The merrymaking continued until everybody was fully drunk. At 3, when they were about to leave, Bhushan took out the *Premier Amour* bottle from his trouser pocket and thrust it towards Bhanu, 'Oh, by the way, Bhanu, you left in such a hurry last evening that I forgot to give this to you. Better late than never.'

Bhanu immediately sobered a bit, 'No, I can't.'

Bhushan sounded surprised, 'Why not? It's just perfume.'

Satish sided with him, 'Oh, come on, Bhanu.'

Bhanu realized she was cornered into accepting it, 'It really was not necessary. Thanks anyway. Good night.'

Once in her room, she unwrapped the bottle and read aloud the name, '*Premier Amour*. Very French, very vogue. But what does it mean?'

She googled the English translation—First Love.

'Clever, smart bastard,' she muttered and whiffed at the bottle's neck.

Rajanigandha! He remembered!

Closing her eyes, she took a slow, deep breath. The feeling was other-worldly, it added to the intoxication of alcohol.

Just then, Bhushan's message had to bleep. She opened her Whatsapp, 'It's your fav—rajanigandha, like it?'

Bhanu replied, 'Why????'

—What do you mean why?

—Why are you doing this?

—I am not doing anything. It's happening on its own.

She did not reply, so he messaged again, 'Our meeting was cut short. There's a lot to talk about. Tomorrow evening, same place?'

—NO, no way.

—Pls.

Bhanu did not reply. He waited for 10 minutes, then gave up and went for a shower. Bhanu's message was waiting on him when he came out, 'The fragrance is still in d air, it's good, where did you get it?'

—It's a long story.

—Make it short and tell me.

—Over dinner tomorrow?

Silence. He could tell she was in two minds, so he pushed it, 'Sure?'

—Maybe.

And he knew she would come.

14

It's All Falling Into Place

Bhanu's hangover was gone by mid-morning the next day. With a clear mind, she seriously reconsidered her dinner date with Bhushan. Would she be sending out a wrong signal to him that she was open to reconciliation? That was out of the question with the other woman in his life. So what was the point in meeting him again?

She typed out a message to Bhushan, 'I don't see any point in meeting again. Thanks for the perfume.'

Before she could send it, her mother's incoming call popped up.

'Mom! How's it going?'

'All good here. And you, beta?'

Bhanu blurted out in a single breath, 'I'm good Maa, on a 24/7 roll. Cannes is amazing, with a jamboree of people from different cultures. And Maa, we had a swell post-awards party last night. And Maa…'

'Yes, I am listening.'

'And Maa, Bhushan is here.'

Mother was instantly alert, 'He? There?'

'He hosted last night's party.'

'What is he doing there? I hope he is not stalking you.'

'No, Maa. It's just a coincidence. He is here for his work

and a bit of leisure.'

'What work?'

'He is extending his store's product line to include perfumes and other fragrances. He is in France to strike franchise deals.'

'You are sounding like his PR manager Bhanu.' Mother remarked.

Bhanu was slightly miffed, 'Well, you asked for the details, Mom.'

'Okay, so?'

Bhanu filled her in on the details. When she was done, mother asked, 'I don't want to be nosy, Bhanu, but I can't help being a mother. So tell me, how would you sum it up?'

'All said and done, Maa, we were exes meeting as friends. He is still very emotional about me, and it's still very real. I realized it because of the personalized perfume he gifted me last night after the party. He's named it *Premier Amour*, and it means First Love. And the fragrance is rajanigandha. He remembers every tiny detail about me. He still cares.'

Mother thought it over and agreed, 'You're right. It's not hollow flattery. One can go to such lengths only when the love is true and the break-up has hurt.'

Bhanu said, 'And after the party, he messaged late in the night to ask if I had liked the perfume. We chatted some, and then he asked me out for dinner tonight.'

Mother completed it for her, 'And you agreed.'

'Sort of, under the effect of a few drinks. But this morning, I rethought. Maa, what's the point of loving someone so deeply when you can't take it to the finishing line? It's got no future. The bottom line is that he is betrothed to another woman.'

Bhanu then remembered her unsent message to Bhushan, 'Oh that reminds me, I was about to WhatsApp him to cancel the dinner when you called…'

Mother interrupted, 'Wait, don't just cancel it yet beta. Let's chat via Skype.'

'Give me ten minutes.'

On Skype, mother came straight to the point, 'Bhanu, two things are very clear. He still loves you as deeply as ever, and he wants you in his life. It's unclear whether he is still engaged, as he mentioned in his email. Why don't you try and find it out tonight?'

'So you're asking me to go for the dinner date. Even if I did, Maa, you know it's not like me to ask him on his face. I'm too righteous. And why should I do that? I have almost got over it. I had made up my mind to cancel the date and wish him good luck in life…'

Mother interrupted, 'And then keep following him on YouTube for the rest of your life? Bhanu, there are some people you can never let go of in life. For you, they are your Paa and Bhushan. You may learn to live without both, but life would be fuller, richer, and infinitely more fulfilling with them. While bringing Paa back is not possible, I feel providence is arranging for you to let Bhushan back in your life. True love is a rarity these days. If it's coming your way, don't let it pass. It's a manifestation from above, just like your friendship with Buddy, and it's just as priceless.'

Bhanu said, 'Even if you are right, I won't be part of a love triangle, and I won't have anything to do with breaking a solemnized betrothal. I am better off being a loser than being a homewrecker.'

'I am just asking you to find out whether he is still engaged or not. You owe it to yourself. Believe me, you will regret it later if it turns out to be a lost chance.'

Bhanu bit her lip, started to say something, then changed her mind and said, 'Tell me something, Maa.'

'What?'

'Why is first love so stubborn? Why doesn't it go away?'

'It's always been that way, beta, ever since man and woman loved for the first time. Don't question first love, just love. Go to the dinner, take your chance.'

~

Bhanu was dressed in a floral skirt and a crème chiffon blouse. Bhushan wore a checked shirt and worn jeans, and unlike the last time, it looked like he was in his element. He got up to greet Bhanu and shook her hand confidently. As she sat, he declared, 'A perfume is a man's friend in need!'

'And a woman's worst weakness,' she smiled and replied. Whiffs of *Premier Amour* spread in the air.

'*Premier Amour*?' Bhushan asked.

'Why ask, when you know?'

'Liked it?'

'Why ask, when you know?'

And they both laughed.

Over the starter drink, Bhushan initiated the talk, 'So, what after the thesis, a job or entrepreneurship?'

'A job initially, and you?'

'My store is my life now.'

Bhanu asked with a hint of admiration, 'How did you manage everything within such a short time?'

'Passion and undivided attention,' Bhushan replied.

Bhanu smiled agreeably. Then she asked, 'So what's your story about *Premier Amour*? I have agreed to this dinner primarily to know about it.'

Bhushan told her about the perfume-making workshop, his choice of fragrance, and the selection of its name. Bhanu controlled a blush, but her eyes smiled nevertheless. He thought she would say something, but she remained lost in her world.

He continued, 'Bhanu, hearts in love conspire in crazy ways to treasure bygone memories. I never stopped loving you despite everything that happened. This perfume gave me a fragrant means to cherish your memories. I had never imagined that I would be presenting it to you in person. It is incredible the way things have developed. This is not a mere coincidence. Something or someone wants us to reunite and is working overtime to make it happen.'

Bhanu felt her mother's predicament echo in Bhushan's words. Aloud, though, she decided to play it differently, 'There is someone else who has the first right to that gift.'

Bhushan got her message and quickly refuted it, 'No, the gift is yours.'

Bhanu drew a big question mark on the table with her finger.

In reply, Bhushan punched his first finger forcefully on the table, indicating a full stop. He said, 'I convinced Brinda that the engagement was an alliance between two friendly families, not between two hearts. I could have never been a good husband to her even if you had never entered my life. She was very upset, but in the end, she understood. The betrothal was called off with her willing consent.'

Relief ran through Bhanu's body like adrenalin. She wanted to jump for joy. At the same time, she felt sorry for Brinda, 'It's unfair to her.'

'In fact, it's the only fair thing I did to her. I freed her from a life of emotional drudgery.'

The attendant appeared, and Bhushan started to order a

4-course meal that would take time to finish.

After the waiter had left, Bhanu said, 'I only hope I was not implicated in all this. Although I don't know your family or Brinda, it affects me even if strangers hold me responsible for things I never did.'

'I didn't let your name get smeared in any way, Bhanu. I fought with mummy and Brinda to uphold your integrity.'

Bhanu felt a sudden rush of fondness for him. He was single again, and still deeply in love with her. He had stood by her at all costs. He had named his business after her and created a special perfume! And now he was wooing her doggedly. Her liking for him was coming back with a vengeance. She loosened up and told herself, *Let me cut him some slack.*

'So, you are young, handsome, successful, self-made, etc., and you are in the lifestyle business. Why are you still single?'

'Who would give a second look at this couch potato?' He ran his hand over his slight paunch..

'Bad try, it gives you an air of affluence. And a fat wallet speaks louder than a lean body.'

That was vintage Bhanu, sharp and spontaneous. Bhushan loved it. He, too, got back in his element.

'Vice versa in my case, fat body and lean wallet.'

'Bad try at modesty.'

And they laughed heartily.

Before they knew it, Bhanu and Bhushan had slipped into their cozy comfort zone. Lost ground was being recovered quickly, without their consciously noticing it.

Food came and they ate unhurriedly. The dinner was turning out to be a dream run, and they went with the flow. It was late when they finally stepped out. The air was chilly, and that gave them an excuse to hold hands. The crowds had thinned by then, and there were lonely swaths on the road that led to their hotel. They stopped at one such dark patch. Bhushan pressed Bhanu's hand, and she responded by clasping it tightly. Something was conveyed to each other in that fleeting moment. They looked up and down the promenade to make sure it was deserted, and then, Bhanu rose on her toes, and they locked their lips. It happened suddenly. Neither of them had seen it coming, but that's how suppressed emotions erupt as spontaneous lust. Not a word was spoken. There was urgency in their kiss as if it had been put off for too long. And it was clumsy, entry-level kissing, but what it lacked in proficiency, it made up with spontaneity.

In the middle of the heat, he asked, 'How's it going?'

'Clumsy but cool' she muttered.

'Cool?' He replied, 'It's smoking fucking hot.'

She corrected him, 'Fucking smoking hot.'

'Just hot.'

He grabbed her again and began to kiss her hungrily.

It continued until moments became minutes, and then time lost its relevance. A police patrol car passing by slowed down but did not interfere. They kissed some more, this time, with more emotion and passion.

At long last, the fever subsided. They walked toward the hotel with a slow, dreamy stride. Before entering the hotel, they stopped and smiled at each other for a moment. Bhanu's face radiated a full-moonish glow. After fighting many inner battles in the past few days, she finally felt at peace with herself. The struggle had ended, and love had won.

Impulsively, Bhanu gave out a low-pitch cry, 'Wwwwooooooohhhhhhhooooooo.'

Thousands of miles away to the east, it echoed amidst the desolate, lofty cliffs of Zanskar, and a lumbering mountain

mumbled in its sleep, 'That must be Bhanu and Bhushan.'
Zanskar 2.0 had begun.

~

In the hotel's lounge, a still-excited Bhushan said, 'The game must go on till the end. Extra time needed.'

Bhanu, 'You have running cold water in the shower, right?'

'Yes, why?'

'Stand under it and cool off, hot-pants. Good night. See ya tomorrow.'

She ruffled his hair and disappeared into the elevator.

~

Bhanu called her mother late next morning, 'A bear hug to the best Maa on earth, what's up?'

Mother deliberately sounded low-energy, 'Managing the chores single-handedly, want to take a year's break after you return.'

'As if I will oblige you. Maa, when can we talk?'

'What are we doing now?'

'I mean serious talk, not small talk.'

'Oh,' her mother switched to serious mode, 'Give me an hour. On Skype. Bye.'

When they Skyped, Bhanu launched her monologue, 'Mum, I went for the dinner date. He has called off the engagement. He said that he would have done so even if we had never met; there was simply no connection between them. Mum, he did not allow muck to be thrown at me. He stood by me firmly, fought with his mother for me. And Maa, he is doing so well with his new venture.'

Then she mellowed, 'And Maa, he hasn't been able to get

over his *Premier Amour.*'

Mother showered her wishes, 'I am truly, enormously glad for you, beta. The Grand Plan for you both seems to be working. May you love and live correctly from now until eternity.'

Then she asked, 'So, what's the plan now?

'Satish is throwing a bash tonight, and tomorrow we are heading to Monaco for a day tour. The day after, I fly back to home sweet home, Mum sweet Mum.'

'Can't wait to hug you,' her mother reciprocated.

Bhushan was also talking to his mother, but the talk was brief and customary. He asked the usual dutiful questions—whether she was keeping well and taking her medicines regularly, whether she needed anything, etc. The call ended in less than 3 minutes, and Bhushan felt a sense of duty having been fulfilled.

~

Satish had made reservations at the bar of an upscale hotel. Their table offered the best panoramic view of the night-time promenade and the sea.

'Guys, drink till you drop,' Satish said, raising his glass.

Bhanu quipped, 'Sure will, Bhushy, may the night last long.'

Bhushy!

It had come out of her mouth suddenly, unintentionally.

Eyeballs rolled. 'Bhushy? WTF! Something's going on behind our backs,' declared one of them.

Bhanu said lamely, 'Oh, it's nothing. We used to call him by that nickname.'

Bhushan was beaming, and alcohol only helped. He proclaimed, 'And guys—guys, her nickname was Bhalu.'

The only other girl in the group rolled her eyes, 'Bhushy and Bhalu, wow! What a pair!'

Bhalu went coy while Bhushy mellowed momentarily.

So the secret was out. Satish got up and announced, 'I hereby declare the love games between Bhushy and Bhalu open!'

Glasses clinked, followed by applause and then endless leg-pulling of the newly discovered couple.

The celebration lasted until the wee hour. The lovebirds trailed the others while walking back to the hotel and pressed hands when they reached the previous night's kissing spot, but history did not repeat, for want of favourable circumstances.

In the elevator, the director asked Bhanu with a wink, 'Fifth floor or second, mademoiselle?' He knew that Bhushan had put up on the second floor.

'Fifth, monsieur,' Bhanu replied, showing a thumbs-down sign to Bhushan.

~

In Monaco, the next day, the group had an overdose of fun and frolic and retired early after returning to Cannes. The next morning, they would be leaving for Paris, and from there, to India. Bhushan had to stay back in Paris to tie some loose ends with two perfumers. While seeing off Bhanu and her team at the airport, he said, 'Okay, guys, I mean it, France has given me five wonderful friends and one more-than-wonderful girlfriend. And, of course, *Premier Amour*. What more can I ask for?'

There were farewell hugs and cheerios. Before releasing Bhanu from his arms, Bhushan said, 'Until this weekend.'

'Until eternity,' Bhanu replied and walked past him without looking back.

I got it right the third time, she mused, as she remembered the previous two occasions on which she had walked past Bhushan.

~

At the airport, Mother greeted Bhanu as only mothers can, with a beaming, broad grin that told Bhanu she was proud of her. They hugged for a full minute and then Mother said, 'Welcome home, my child.'

'Home is where mom's hugs are.'

Bhanu chattered non-stop while going home. There was no order in her talk, she began by saying that the food on the flight was awful and she was hungry, then she narrated their lovely Monaco visit, then jumped to the award ceremony, then to the wild celebration, and so on. Finally, she touched upon Bhushan, 'Maa, he is a cool guy. Success has not changed him.'

'That speaks volumes about his upbringing, sanskaar, Bhanu. Some families absorb wealth and fame like a sponge—they don't let affluence spill.'

Then she nudged Bhanu and winked, 'Whoever Bhushan marries is going to be a lucky girl.'

Bhanu, 'Lucky, my foot. He should thank his lucky stars that I let him in my life again.'

Mother, 'So, the deal is sealed?'

'200 per cent'

'We are meeting in Delhi this weekend. He wants me to visit his store and meet his mother.'

'Happy dating,' Mother teased.

And Bhanu went pink all over her face.

15

The Forever Journey Begins

Bhanu's flight to Delhi was delayed. Bhushan complained when they met, 'You're late, darling.'

'The best things in life arrive a bit late,' she said, and gave him a long, approving look.

'You look horrible, read adorable.'

'You look pretty, read desirable.'

'Perv.'

As they settled in the car, Bhushan took her hands and kissed each palm lingeringly.

Bhanu said, 'Missed you. Is it just four days since our last date?'

Bhushan laughed and then added, 'Oh, by the way, we're going home. I've had a talk with Mom about us. It's all right for you to put up at my place.'

Bhanu was taken aback; Bhushan had not mentioned anything about it to her earlier. She sounded a bit annoyed, 'You should have asked me before deciding on your own, Bhushy. It's the first time we're meeting like this. I don't know anyone else in your family…'

Bhushan sought to cut her off, 'You know me, and that's all that matters. It's okay, chill.'

Bhanu countered him, 'No, it's not okay, Bhushy. Try to see

my point. It hasn't been too long since your engagement was called off, and you want me to walk into your home as your girlfriend. What will people think? What will your mother think? That the match was fixed. No Bhushy, I'm not comfortable with this at all—I—I've told you once before, I get buggered even if strangers think wrongly about me.'

She paused before continuing, 'Look, Bhushy, I will gladly meet your mother, but staying at your place the very first time around? Come on, you shouldn't have decided for me.'

Bhushan pondered for a moment, then conceded, 'Okay.'

He called his mother and briefly told her about the change in the plan. Mother said something about it being a disappointment, and he replied that Bhanu had a very close friend in Delhi who insisted she stay with her. Mother then asked Bhushan to bring home Bhanu for dinner, and he 'Sure, Mom.'

Turning to Bhanu, Bhushan asked, 'Where to, now?'

She demanded, 'Take me to the best hotel in town.'

~

As they sipped coffee in the lounge, Bhanu asked, 'So, what's the plan?'

'To make the most of your decision to stay in a hotel,' Bhushan winked.

'Keep your hands off me, or else…' she clawed her fingers and Bhushan laughed.

However, they ended up being in her room after half an hour. Both of them had sensed it coming in the lounge. Bhushan kicked the door shut. Instantly, they were clenching each other in a passionate embrace and helping each other undress.

~

Physical connections create a great bonding of hearts. The bodies, as manifests of love, become eager to give and take. There is a tearing rush to own and disown, to gain and lose, to be and not to be. It's like the confluence of two stormy seas that ultimately creates one serene ocean, and the waters become calm and one.

Such love goes into the making of all civilizations. Sex may find newer means and methods of heightening sensual pleasure in this age of innovation and experimentation, but good old lovemaking will never be out of fashion. It creates legends in every era and every culture—Romeo and Juliet, Odysseus and Penelope, Sohni and Mahiwal, Tarzan and Jane.

~

'Hey, Tarzan, I'm famished,' Bhanu said lazily, sprawling under the blanket, her voice spent but content.

'Food is right in front of you,' Bhushan pointed a finger at himself.

'I'm done with hot and spicy stuff. I want a sweet dish now.'

She raised herself and kissed Bhushan fondly, then said, 'Now feed me some real food. And please get me some water.'

Bhushan got out of the bed to get water.

Room service delivered food, and they ate mouthfuls hungrily. When they were done eating, Bhushan raised an eyebrow, 'Now you have energy?'

'Sex maniac,' Bhanu said and cuddled up to him.

At the end of it, they lay in each other's arms, too exhausted to speak, their eyes and hands doing the talking. Feeling completely at home in each other's arms, they slipped into a deep, sound sleep.

Bhanu woke up after what seemed like ages. She woke

up with a start and nudged Bhushan, 'Bhushy wake up. It's already dark.'

He replied sleepily, 'It's still dark. Sleep baby, and let me sleep.'

'Oye, moron, it's dark as in the late evening and not early morning.'

She checked the time and jumped, 'OMG, it's 8:20! We slept for over three hours. Bhushy, get up, we have to go to your home for dinner.'

Bhushan was up instantly, 'Fuck, yeah, baby.'

He checked his phone, which was on silent mode. His mother had already called thrice. He called back and kept it short, 'Hello, Mum. Yeah, it's me. Sorry, we are a bit late. We are reaching there by 9:20.'

~

Bhanu was dressed in a knee-length floral skirt and a matching pastel blouse, with a scarf around her neck. As Bhushan's mother opened the door, Bhanu smiled amiably, covered her head with the scarf and bowed, saying, 'Pranam, Auntyji, how are you?'

Bhushan was stumped by Bhanu's sudden sobriety but masked his surprise behind a square face. His mother gave Bhanu a long, approving look and said, 'Live long, beti.'

Then she welcomed her into the home, 'Come.'

Bhanu took the first step gingerly as the implication of entering that house dawned on her, but she gained confidence with each step. As they sat, she felt at ease, as if it was a familiar place, as if she belonged there. First thing, Bhushan's mother offered Bhanu a piece of jaggery to sweeten her mouth, as was the tradition.

'Beti, have something sweet.'

'Thanks, Auntyji' Bhanu reciprocated the gesture, offering back a piece to her. She accepted it and smiled, 'Come, sit. Feel at home.'

Bhanu nodded. She did feel comfortable already, thanks to the genuine and heart-warming welcome. She had noticed that just for a fleeting second, Bhushan's mother had compared her with Brinda at the door, but then she had quickly come to terms with the reality and willingly accepted her into the family. She developed an instant liking for Bhushan's mother. She may be a bit stereotypical, she thought, but she is noble and pure-hearted; she won't nurse a grudge against me.

After some small talk, mother said, 'Come, let's have dinner.'

It was a Punjabi feast meant as much to impress an important guest as to appease the taste buds. Bhanu was more than impressed. There were three richly buttered Punjabi vegetables afloat in aromatic spicy curry, two sweets—jalebis fried in pure ghee and thick kesar kheer, then there was kaju khoya and shahi rajma, Punjabi samosa, raita, tadka daal and jeera rice, and of course, buttered roti and stuffed paratha were to be served straight off the pan while they ate.

Bhushan's mother sat Bhanu beside her and said fondly, 'Beti, please start.'

Bhanu said almost in wonderment, 'Auntyji, this is just too big a spread.'

'Arre, beti you have not even started yet,' and she started serving Bhanu. A light eater, Bhanu was aghast at the portions that were being dumped on her plate. She kept refusing, and Bhushan's mother kept insisting on serving more. Ultimately, Bhushan had to intervene, 'Mom, Bhanu can't finish all this even in five meals. It will all go waste. It's better if you let her serve herself.'

For a moment, mother looked offended, but she quickly made light of it, 'Youngsters these days are such light eaters! Okay, then, serve yourself. I will just say, eat until you can't eat anymore!' And then she laughed at her own humour.

'Sure, I will,' Bhanu laughed and reassured her.

Bhushan and his mother ate heartily, and Bhanu had to nibble at her food until they were finished. Then mother asked for dessert, 'Shankar, bring the kulfi.'

And Bhanu went into a tizzy, 'What? There is still kulfi to come?!'

'Haan, beti, you must have something sweet.'

'Auntyji, please, I can't even drink water now.'

Bhushan came to her rescue once again, 'Mom, please don't force Bhanu'

And mother sighed, 'Okay. I hope you did not remain hungry.'

And Bhanu gave out a hearty laugh, 'Hungry? I am sure I won't feel hungry for three days.'

After dinner, Bhushan's mother asked Bhanu some customary questions about her family, her roots, her maternal lineage, whether she would like to continue working after marriage, and so on. It was more to satisfy herself that she had 'interviewed' her future daughter-in-law than of any real consequence. Bhanu gave her replies amiably and patiently, and Bhushan heaved a sigh of relief. After a while, he glanced at his watch and said to Bhanu, 'It's 11:30. Your friend will be waiting for you.'

Bhanu picked it up from there, 'Auntyji, I hate to go but I don't want to be too late in reaching my friend's place. Thank you so very much. I really enjoyed it. The food was delicious, and I am overwhelmed by your heartfelt welcome.'

As she rose to leave, mother said, 'One minute, beti.'

She went into the bedroom and returned with an envelope, 'Beti, this is for you.'

Bhanu was taken aback; the cover contained a thick wad of currency notes, 'Oh no, Auntyji, I cannot take this, no, please. Your blessings are all that I—we need.'

Bhushan's mother's eyes moistened a bit as she said, 'Beti, it is a custom. It is not money. You don't know how much love and affection there is behind each note. If you refuse this, I will feel very bad.'

Bhushan knew that his mother had reached a tipping point. He signalled Bhanu to accept the envelope.

Mother was happy.

Before leaving, Bhanu started to bow to Bhushan's mother, but she took her in her arms.

Bhanu felt as if she was being hugged by her own mother. In that moment, their acceptance of each other became complete.

On the way back, Bhushan asked Bhanu a bit tentatively, 'How was mother?'

Bhanu replied confidently, 'Super cool.'

That loosened up Bhushan, 'And your would-be hubby? Is he cool too?'

'Nope. He's smoking hot,' and she bent and kissed Bhushan's cheek.

When they reached the hotel, Bhushan looked at Bhanu, 'How 'bout a repeat of the evening?'

'Your mother would smell a scandal if you're late in reaching home. I want to retain my clean image, yet.'

Bhushan said in a resigned tone, 'Okayyyy.'

Both whispered, 'Good night,' almost at the same time.

She got out of the car and breezed away, 'Tomorrow, take me to your store.'

No sooner than Bhanu had entered her room, her phone rang. It was Buddy. She jumped for joy, 'Buddy, my darling devil! How cool of you to have called! Where are you and how are you and why no contact for so long?'

'Hiiiiiii' Buddy tried to sound stylish, 'Bhanu! No, no, nothing like that, in fact, I am so excited to speak to you! How are you? I am in Gangtok only and have passed my B.Com, so I thought I would let you know.'

'Great to know Buddy, congratulations and a big hug. So now you are literally an eligible bachelor!'

Buddy was smug. He laughed, 'You are joking, Bhanu. Any ways, I had called your home first and spoke to Aunty. She told me you are in Delhi. When I asked her why you had gone to Delhi, she avoided answering and said that I should speak to you to find out. So what's the matter Bhanu, I hope everything is all right?'

'It's all good, Buddy. Don't worry. I am on cloud nine.'

'Means?'

'Oh, I mean, I feel like I'm on top of the world. I am in love.'

Buddy exclaimed, 'Oh?! That's a big surprise. I am so happy for you. Who is the lucky person?'

'It's the same Bhushy bastard.'

Buddy felt a mixture of confusion and slight annoyance, as he said, 'Oh no, he was already engaged. I thought you had got over him?'

'I thought so too, Buddy. But then he reentered my life through a string of crazy flukes after calling off his engagement, and he convinced me that he still loved me very deeply. I, too, realized that I would not be able to love anyone else as I had loved him. Ultimately, first love got the better of me.'

Then she added playfully, 'And after all, a known bastard is better than an unknown gentleman.'

Buddy could not accept it readily, 'I still can't believe this Bhanu; it sounds so unreal. You better tell me the whole story.'

And so Bhanu gave him a recap of Zanskar 2.0.

She took almost twenty minutes to tell it all to Buddy, and both of them laughed heartily when Bhanu narrated the details of the lavish dinner earlier that evening.

Then, on an impulse, she asked, 'Buddy, will you talk to Bhushy?'

'How?'

'Wait,' Bhanu said and started a conference call with Bhushan, 'Bhushy, it's Buddy on the third end, Buddy—talk to Bhushy.'

'Hi, Bhushan! I am Baldev, Bhanu's Buddy. How are you doing?'

'Hey, dude! I am doing great, what about you? I have heard a lot about you from Bhanu. She really treasures your friendship.'

'Yeah, we are very good friends. I feel lucky to have Bhanu…'

'Careful there, she is mine,' Bhushan joked and then added quickly, 'Just joking, dude.'

They talked for some fifteen minutes. After the call, Bhanu stretched out on the bed, overcome with gratitude toward whoever made it all happen for her. She thought, I have the world's best BF and BFF, and it filled her with joy and pride.

~

The Next morning, Bhushan took Bhanu to the store. Late Bhanu Pratap Singh's larger-than-life portrait covered the wall facing the entrance. Below the portrait, a line bearing Bhushan's signature read, 'You live here, in every atom of this place. Lead, Kindly Light.'

Bhushan looked up at the portrait. Gesturing at Bhanu, he said, 'Dad, your daughter-in-law, ooppss sorry, your daughter.'

Bhanu came forward and folded her hands. It was the first time she was seeing Bhushan's father. His easy smile and kind features mirrored his clean heart. Bhanu felt that he must have been a person who wouldn't have wronged anybody knowingly in his life.

'How's dad?' Bhushan whispered to her.

'Super cool,' Bhanu whispered back.

Then she noticed the striking similarities between father and son—the same strong jawline, handsome long face, chiselled sharp nose, a disarming smile, the rich mane of jet-black hair, and dimpled right cheek. She joked to Bhushan, 'I now know how you will look in your later years, when Bunty and Babli will grow up.'

At last, she had let her guard down and allowed herself the thought of bearing Bhushan's children. Standing there in the shelter of Bhanu Pratap Singh, she truly felt like family.

~

Once in his cabin, Bhushan asked Bhanu to take his seat, 'You belong here; the store bears your name.'

Bhanu was overwhelmed, 'Oh no, I can't, I have not done anything to earn that seat. No drama, Bhushy, you sit there,' she insisted and quickly took a seat across the table.

After coffee, Bhushan took Bhanu around.

The store was spread over three floors of sprawling retail space. The ground floor housed men's section, while the first floor was dedicated to women's collections.

'Women on top,' Bhanu quipped.

'Make it singular, and tonight,' Bhushan responded with his quick wit.

'Perv,' Bhanu repeated her favourite slang for Bhushan.

Half of the second floor was occupied by accessories, sportswear and adventure gear, while Bhushan had earmarked the other half for the fragrance section.

Bhanu loved the interior décor, floor layouts, and arrangement of merchandise. Moreover, the sales and customer care staff were trained not to breathe down the customers' necks but to help them make better choices. The tour was a fantastic experience for Bhanu. She thought, *It is so mindful of the shoppers and their needs that they would be addicted to this place.* Back in Bhushan's cabin, she complimented him, 'Congratulations. I am truly proud of you, Bhushy. You have put your heart into this place.'

'This place is my second love. Without it, I could not have overcome the first one.'

'Now you have both.'

'Lucky me.'

Often, pride in one's lover's achievements finds an outlet in passionate love games in bed. Bhanu felt an instant, powerful need to possess Bhushan. Bhushan cancelled the late lunch order and simply said to her, 'Come.'

They made primal, greedy love at the hotel, shedding all niceties. Later, lying in Bhushan's arms, Bhanu said, 'Now I know what it is like to be loved in absolute terms.'

'Me too.'

When they had caught their breaths, they managed a quickie before it was time for Bhanu's flight. At the airport, he told her, 'Don't go.'

'Don't let me go,' she replied.

But she did go—only to meet him in Mumbai the next weekend.

When they met at the Mumbai airport, Bhanu told Bhushan, 'I have a surprise for you.'

'What?' Bhushan was eager to know.

She raised her ring finger to show him a cute 'B&B' tattooed on its side. The etching was fresh, the swelling still showed.

Bhushan was overcome with love and hugged Bhanu tightly.

When they broke their hug, Bhanu raised her middle finger, 'Actually, you deserve this.'

Bhushan let out a shriek of laughter. The tone was set for a fun-filled weekend.

The relationship had settled now, like how a muddy, volatile monsoon brook calms down in spring. All their insecurities had been laid to rest. They loved with absolute faith and trust in each other. Great sexual compatibility made things even better. There was no sense of compromise even in bed. The weekend did not disappoint them.

Bhushan had put up at Bhanu's home. When she went to show him the guest room, there were hurried, half-hearted attempts at intimacy. Kissing Bhushan hastily, Bhanu said, 'Welcome to your sasuraal.'

'Thanks, but I miss the benefits of a hotel.'

'Perv.'

'Try to sneak in late at night.'

'No ways, hot-pants.'

'Skype with me then.'

'Great idea. But for now, dinner is waiting. Come as soon as possible.'

Dinner was not as elaborate as in Delhi, but they ate merrily. Bhanu's mother and Bhushan had connected very well. Over fruits after dinner, they made some more small talk and retired around ten.

At 10:30 sharp, she appeared on his screen in a sleeveless black vest and khaki shorts, no bra. It was the first time Bhushan was seeing her in nightwear. Gaping at her, he exclaimed, 'WTF! I have a sexy girlfriend.'

'Too hot to handle?'

'As hot as red chillies.'

'Ha! You're not burning your mouth this weekend, though.'

Even in hushed tones, their voices seemed to spill out of the rooms, so they switched to typing messages.

—So, mister, missing me?

—That's the understatement of the year.

—Craving for me?

—Another understatement.

—Hhmm how about pulling your hair yearning for me?

—That's closer but not close enough.

—K final try, missing me enough to kill for me?

—Missing you enough to die for you.

That caused sudden lust in Bhanu. 'Keep your door ajar' she typed and signed out of Skype. Tiptoeing into the guest room, she was in Bhushan's arms the next minute. His masculine scent and the strength of his grasp set her on fire, 'Let's create our own Zanskar, *N*ow.'

Bhanu cuddled up to Bhushan in the crammed single bed when it was over and said, 'I miss Zanskar. I wish there were high mountains and tons of snow all around us.'

'And millions of low-hanging stars all above us. But jeez! Don't ask me to pluck them for you.'

She played with his chest and smiled silly, 'It's every girl's right to make such unreasonable demands from her boyfriend when she's taking a huge risk sleeping with him right under the nose of her mother.'

'Ha! I only hope your mother is not an insomniac.'

And Bhanu giggled. She stroked Bhushan's chin, 'Hey, I have to make a confession.'

'That I have competition?'

'No, you're beyond competition, my macho man.'

'Second guess, Uuumm…you're preggy?'

'Shut up, or I'll leave the room.'

'Okay, okay, I give up, you tell me.'

Bhanu became pensive, 'I followed you on YouTube and TV after we broke up. Purely by coincidence, I stumbled upon the live telecast of your store's launch and did not blink until the end. I must say, your speech was crisp. In those thirty-odd minutes that the telecast lasted, you became the object of envy, a celebrity, and I hated you for that. But the more I hated you, the more I missed you. In the days that followed, I tried hard to erase your image from my mind, but somehow you kept coming back at me. I resisted the temptation to Google your name countless times, but the yearning to get your glimpse was too strong. Later, it became a daily habit.'

Bhanu paused and heaved a deep sigh, 'In plain words, Bhushy, I had been stalking you on the internet. I have 61 downloads in the folder named BBS on my Google Drive. That was my secret rendezvous whenever I missed you and wanted to meet you.'

Bhanu had become vulnerable in love. Bhushan felt the need to lighten her up, 'Madam, stalking is a punishable crime.'

'Punish me, then.'

The punishment lasted until four in the morning. Back in her room at dawn, Bhanu slept like a log.

~

On Sunday, they went to a beach island. Their banter lasted until they had driven past the city's fringes and entered the lush serenity of the outskirts. Bhanu was driving. She had to manage the steering with one hand for a while as Bhushan held the other one and did not let it go. He kissed and bit the palm every other minute until Bhanu prompted, 'Bhushy, you're stuck with the palm and missing the real fun. There are a million better spots to kiss me.'

So Bhushan let go of her hand, kissed her at twenty other places, and asked, 'Happy?'

She wanted more and said so. He decided to be unobliging, 'My turn now. I'll drive as you make your mark on me.'

'I can do better than that,' she replied, took to a dirt road off the highway and parked at a clearing camouflaged by thick overgrowth. Mid-way through their lovemaking, they spotted a monkey watching them intently from a distance, eyes narrowed and forehead wrinkled in rapt attention, as if trying to take a leaf or two from the spectacle unfolding before its eyes.

'Shall we give him an open-door performance?' Bhushan said.

'It's a she,' Bhanu corrected him.

'Now I understand her nosy nature.'

'Shut up and focus on your monkey business.'

And Bhushan did just that.

The monkey was emboldened and let out a shriek, and within a minute, her troop joined her. They came closer to get a better view.

'Now we're performing to a full audience,' Bhushan said.

'You better live up to their expectations and mine. You've been a lousy lover today, so far...'

That seemingly hurt Bhushan's ego, 'Watch out,' he said and immersed in power-play.

After it was over, he asked Bhanu, 'How was it?'

'Best yet, I didn't know monkeys turned you on more than me.'

They laughed out loud, had something to drink while they caught their breaths, and fed the monkeys bananas. The monkeys grabbed the fruit like teens attacking popcorn during intermission and waited eagerly for the movie to resume.

The beach was overcrowded with Sunday revellers, most of them being couples. Bhanu was disappointed, 'It's as crowded as Bhuleshwar.'

'We've had our fun. Let them have theirs,' Bhushan replied.

They strolled on the palm-shaded fringes of the beach and kept walking until they reached an isolated patch. Bhanu got an idea, 'Hey Bhushy, let's write our wedding invitations on the sand!'

Bhushan knew that Bhanu's weird ideas peaked when she was on an emotional high. He said enthusiastically, 'Deal! You first.'

Bhanu wrote a paper draft and showed it to Bhushan, 'Dear Mr Bhushan Bhanu Pratap Singh, you are cordially invited to marry Miss Bhanu Gajendraprasad Bhutia, provided you stick to the terms and conditions laid out by her. If not, you can go to hell. Yours sincerely, Bhanu.'

'Wow! I'm touched,' Bhushan said, 'But it's too long. Let's stick to single-line invitations.'

So Bhanu revised her draft, 'Bhushy, Marry me and merry me.'

How could anybody in love deny that invitation?

'Your turn now,' Bhanu said.

And Bhushan etched on the sand, 'Bhanu, marry me in this life and for seven lives.'

Bhanu was touched beyond words but she made a face, 'Such a cheapskate! So you want to marry me seven times with a one-time expense.'

And Bhushan burst out laughing.

Over food in the late evening, they discussed their marriage plans more seriously. Bhanu said, 'Bhushy, I want a basic wedding. Let's keep it simple.'

Bhushan pondered. He was a bit concerned about his mother and relatives, 'I agree, but it's going to be a groom's wedding in our extended family after some 20 years. Mum has huge plans, and relatives are hell-bent on a mega Punjabi marriage. Plus, in dad's absence, mum will feel let down, side-lined, if we do it totally in our way. We will have to strike a balance.'

Bhanu, 'Can't we reason it out with mum?' It's a very personal thing, Bhushy. I can understand merry-making, but what has pomp and blatant display of wealth got to do with a wedding?'

'Agree again. I hope we can convince mum without causing her major heartache.'

'Don't worry, I will charm her,' Bhanu said.

Then she got another weird idea, and her eyes widened with excitement, 'Bhushy, you're gonna love this!'

'Now what?'

She bowled straight in the block-hole, 'Let's get married in Gangtok!'

'Gangtok???!!!' There were multiple question marks and

exclamation marks on Bhushan's face.

Bhanu was ready with her defence, 'Why not? It's my original home. That place is infinitely better than Mumbai; like, your baraat won't get stuck in traffic jams and keep me waiting endlessly. And there is Buddy in Gangtok. And ehm ehm, the best part, you'll save on honeymoon cost—marriage-cum-honeymoon in Gangtok.'

Bhushan's response, 'So you're doling out a buy-one-get-one-free offer? Pay for the marriage and get a honeymoon free. Whoa!'

'Something like that,' Bhanu was still high on her idea.

'But I had French Riviera in mind for the honeymoon.'

'We'll do that after the Gangtok honeymoon naa darling.'

'Wow it's my lucky day! Two honeymoons for one marriage.'

'Happy?'

'Sort of.'

And Bhanu knew he had bought her idea.

'We will have to take mummy in confidence about this, though.' Bhushan, 'Yes, I reckon that. We will combine it with the simple-marriage pitch.'

'Not bad,' she agreed.

It was dark by the time they left for the city. On the way, an army of fireflies suddenly swarmed their path. Bhanu sprung up in sheer delight. She opened the car windows to let them in.

'They look like tiny illuminated angels!' Bhanu exclaimed and started counting them, 'One-two-three-seven-10…'

'What are you counting?' he asked.

'Our blessings.'

~

Mother had prepared momos with chutney and spiced rice for dinner and a dessert pudding. Bhushan and Bhanu told Mother about their wedding plans while eating. She approved both the ideas, 'That's a welcome change, but we will have to take Bhushan's mummy's consent first.'

Bhanu replied, 'But of course, Maa. I suggest you call her up to give it a formal touch.'

Then the talk switched to the wedding date.

Bhushan said, 'A summer wedding, of course.'

'Sometime in April or May?' Bhanu's mother asked.

'Yesss!' Bhanu was perked up, 'By that time, Gangtok would be at its glorious best.'

Then Bhanu's mother asked, 'We should take your mother's opinion before anything is finalized. Is it all right if I call her tomorrow night?'

'Yes, that'll be fine,' Bhushan said, and they called it a day.

~

Bhushan called Bhanu after 15 minutes, 'Hi, still awake?'

'No I'm fast asleep. This is my ghost speaking'

'Hey, ghostji, I just realized something.'

'Like what?'

'I haven't officially proposed to you yet.'

'Oh that, well, you better do that before I change my mind.'

He proposed to her in Delhi the next weekend. Keeping in mind their Gangtok wedding, he had chosen a restaurant with an ethnic Himalayan menu. He had kept the proposal idea simple but original. After ordering food, he opened the website www.marrymeandmerryme.com on his tablet and showed it to Bhanu. The screen had tuberose stems falling randomly from the top of the screen and gathering in a pile at the base. When the pile was sufficiently dense, Bhushan's proposal got etched on it:

Bhanu, marry me for seven lives.

Mist formed in Bhanu's eyes. Bhushan took both her hands in his and mouthed the words 'marry me' without speaking them. She nodded coyly, eyes now brimming and tiny arches forming at the edges of her lips as she smiled. Flashing his dimpled smile as if in reply to hers, he asked, 'Deal?'

Still too emotional to speak, she showed him a thumbs-up sign and surfed the website further.

Two animated platinum rings appeared on the screen on the next page and began to dance. As they came close, they smooched, and a callout appeared, 'Deal is sealed!' By then, Bhanu had found her voice. She joked, 'Where's my real ring, you miser?

Bhushan took out a platinum band from a beautiful leather box and slipped it onto Bhanu's ring finger. It had a tiny B&B etched on it, done in the same style as Bhanu's tattoo. She said, 'The two have become one.'

Bhushan got up, kneeled, and kissed the ring, 'Marry me, Bhanu.'

'I will,' She nodded.

Bhushan showed Bhanu the next page of the website.

'Wedding Invitation' the page read. The line was superimposed on a collage of their beach photos, and below it was written, 'RSVP.'

Bhanu smiled fondly at his wit, 'I'm coming.'

'Me too' Bhushan replied.

The next few pages were a wishful mosaic of their married life. There was the wedding page that visualized Bhanu and Bhushan in traditional wedding costumes performing the rites. Then there was the honeymoon page in the riviera setting. Looking at it, Bhanu asked, 'Are you sure about the riviera, baby?'

Bhushan replied, 'But of course,' and then as an afterthought,

'Or do you have any more weirdness up your sleeve?'

Bhanu's face lit up, and she exclaimed, 'Idea!'

Bhushan's face dimmed with despair, 'Now what?'

Unmindful of his lack of enthusiasm, she moved to the edge of her chair and said excitedly, 'Zanskar, that's what! Let's honeymoon in Zanskar!'

'Gosh, Bhanu give me a break. Everything is frigid there. 24/7/365'.

'I'm sure it's not true. Zanskar in May should be a totally different scene. Even Antarctica has a milder climate once a year. I'm excited, inspired, perked up, etc. etc. I'm gonna find out more.'

Bhushan shrugged noncommittally, but Bhanu knew he was already latched on to the idea. He went back to showing her the rest of the website.

The next page had the sketch of a pregnant Bhanu, and then the arrivals of Bunty and Babli, and then Bhanu and Bhushan aging gracefully into their plump fifties, and finally, the old-age couple with grey hair and slowed strides and hunched backs.

Closing the website, Bhushan said, 'Until death does us apart.'

Bhanu reminded him, 'The deal is for seven lives.'

Dinner was delectable, and the icing on the cake that was that evening was a complimentary dessert by the restaurant management. It was a tall glass of real mint with vanilla float, a more-than-perfect ending to a perfect evening.

~

Bhanu's mother accompanied her to Delhi. The would-be mothers-in-law also hit it off very well that evening, and had a great time shopping, eating and making merry.

Over breakfast on Sunday, they discussed the wedding date. Bhushan's mother was a staunch believer in astrology, and so she called on the family pundit. After detailed calculations, he pronounced that the full moon day of 4 May would be ideal for the wedding ceremony. Bhanu jumped for joy, exclaiming like a child, 'A summer wedding on a full-moon evening in Gangtok, wow, dream wedding!'

Bhushan's mother immediately brought six types of sweets to celebrate, 'Here, let's share some sweets.'

And sweetness spread in the entire room.

Bhanu called Buddy, 'Budds! It's on the fourth of May!'

Buddy did not get her, 'Hi Bhanu, what is on the fourth of May?'

'My wedding with Bhushan in Gangtok. Didn't I tell you that you'll be the first to know?'

Buddy was delighted, 'Oh great! I am so excited to know Bhanu. Congratulations. I will take care of all the preparations here, don't worry.'

'Thanks, Budds, but it's going to be a low-key wedding. No hullabaloo. We want to keep it quiet and private.'

Buddy's excitement was punctured, 'Oh ok, if that's what you want.'

They talked some more about the wedding, and then Buddy said, 'Bhanu, it is really, really great to hear today's news. I am eagerly waiting for the big day.'

'Me too, Buddy, and thanks in advance for all your help that I'm going to need,' Bhanu replied.

'What are friends for Bhanu? Don't say thanks.'

Bhanu ended the call with warmth, 'Okay, Budds, remote hugs, catch up later.'

At the airport that evening, Bhushan picked up a wristwatch

to gift to Bhanu.

'What's this for?' She asked.

'To remind you that every time it ticks, my heart will beat for you,' he replied, mimicking a famous Bollywood voice.

'Very filmy. So you'll miss me sixty times in a minute,' she said.

'I wish there were more seconds in a minute,' he replied.

She brushed his unruly hair, 'Super filmy.'

~

The next weeks were very active for Bhanu and Bhushan. While she was busy catching up with the coursework of a journalism programme that she had joined recently, he was busy giving final touches to the fragrance section in his store. Any more weekend dates were out of the question, but they kept up with their Skype dates. Bhanu discussed the final draft of her assignments with Bhushan. He showed her the photos of the in-progress fragrance section and took her inputs. They showed each other the things they had bought for their wedding and honeymoon. They even finalized the name of the fragrance section on Skype. Out of all the options, they zeroed in on 'FRA', which Bhanu found cute, stylish, and easy to become fond of.

FRA was inaugurated on April 4. The guests included a known personalities from Delhi's high society. After all, who does not shop for perfumes? The French collaborators were present; it was a gateway to the Indian market for them. Seated in the first row, the two would-be mothers-in-law chatted casually, waiting for the brief event to begin. Brinda and her family were also invited. As they entered the venue, Bhushan's mother rose to greet them warmly. Buddy was busy overseeing buffet arrangements backstage. Soon, Bhanu and Bhushan came to the dais and greeted the guests. As Bhushan took the microphone, the exotic fragrance of *Premier Amour* was released in the air by the event management company.

'Ladies and Gentlemen, Today, we are excited to launch FRA, the Wonderland of French Fragrances, a connoisseur's collection of the finest scents in the world. FRA is a comprehensive range of bath, body and atmospheric scents for all occasions, aromatic products like candles and air fresheners, and much more. We have created a sprawling dedicated shopping space for this venture, offering an array of choices. We welcome you to explore and discover your exotic, personal scent from this collection, which will become your perfume statement.'

Then Bhushan looked straight at the cameras, 'A fragrance has endless possibilities. It can do amazing things. It can help you find your love and start your own fairytale. I should know. Mine was started that way, with *Premier Amour*, whose exotic whiff you can smell all around you. Friends, allow me to introduce my Premiere Amour, my first love Bhanu, the co-creator of this venture.'

There was a long applause. Both the mothers stood up, and the audience followed suit. Bhushan and Bhanu thanked everyone repeatedly with a courteous bow. It was some ten minutes before mingling and merriment began.

At the buffet, Buddy spotted Brinda and easily mistook her for the Bollywood star Rasmi. Bewitched, starry-eyed, nervous, he approached her. Brinda's back was turned to him.

'Excuse me, Rasmi ma'am, can I have a selfie with you?'

She turned and burst out laughing. Heads turned too. Up close, Buddy realized he had created a blunder. Flushed with embarrassment, he started apologizing profusely, 'Oh, sorry, madam, please excuse me. I thought you were Rasmiji and I am her fan…'

Still smiling, Brinda put a reassuring hand on Buddy's shoulder and said, 'It's okay, not your fault. It happens with me.'

People were still paying attention to the small incident. Buddy insisted on owning up the faux pas, 'No, no, it's my fault, madam. I caused you so much embracement.'

Brinda could make out that he meant embarrassment. She again sought to put him at ease, 'I assure you I am not embarrassed, no damage done, I am good, now smile.'

There was something about him which Brinda liked immediately. His innocence? His candour? The sweet pahadi dialect that mashed so well with his naturally robust, macho looks? Whatever it was, Brinda was disarmed by this man who had just 'embraced' her. She offered him, 'Do you still want a selfie?'

That finally relaxed Buddy, and she clicked their friendly selfie on her phone.

'Thank you, madam,' Buddy said

'Brinda,' she introduced herself and extended her hand.

Buddy froze. So this was Brinda. Despite himself, he could not understand why or how Bhushan, anyone, could *not* like her. He was a bit delayed in shaking her hand.

'I am Baldev, Bhanu's best friend.'

After a few awkward moments he started to leave, 'Nice meeting you, Brinda. Please send me the selfie.'

Then he turned around and said, 'Take care, Brinda'

And she knew that he knew who she was.

Her face paled for a moment, but she quickly recovered her regal poise, 'You too, Baldev.'

~

Three days later, Bhanu received a call from a strange number. Thinking that it was spam or a scam, she was about to cut the call when curiosity got the better of her. As she said hello, the voice from the other end beamed, 'Memshaab Juleyy.'

Bhanu jumped. She screeched like a squirrel, 'Tsering! Juleyy! What a surprise! How did you think of calling me today?!'

Tsering, too, was overjoyed, 'Yesh, memshaab, I shuddenly remember you today so calling you today.'

'I am so happy, Tsering! So, where are you and how are you?'

'I am very phine memshaab, I am in Leh now. How are you?'

'I am also very fine, Tsering. So, how come you called?'

'Memsaab I saw you on TV. You have become such a big man.'

Bhanu loved his gender gaffe, 'Oh, no Tsering, nothing like that, it just happened by chance.'

'Memshaab Bhushan Shaab was with you also?'

Then Bhanu understood why he had called. He was puzzled how Bhushan had reentered her life. He was concerned. He wanted to find out. He was not being nosy, he actually cared.

She replied, 'Yes, I was with Bhushy for the opening of his perfume shop.'

'But memsaab...' Tsering let his response linger.

So she tried to put his worry at rest, 'Tsering, you are wondering how come we are together again, right? So listen, we have patched up, we are in love again. You don't worry, everything is fine this time. Bhushy is a gem of a guy.'

That relieved Tsering. He tried his naive humour, 'So memsaab, ilu ilu between you two again.'

She blushed, 'Yes, you can say that.'

'Memsaaab, when is wedding?'

'On the fourth of May in Gangtok, my native place, and

you are coming.'

'I will shurely visit, memshaab.'

Then mischief got the better of her, 'Don't come without a nice gift.'

'Very shurely memshaab, I will ask mother to make a nice shawl for you.'

That had Bhanu doting over him, 'My sweet Tsering.'

Just then, Bhushan called her so she said her goodbye to Tsering, 'Okay then, Tsering, do come for the wedding, I will be waiting.'

~

A total of eleven people were to go to Gangtok for the wedding. Bhushan wanted to keep the number in single digits, but his mother's only sister was unrelenting, and there was also Tsering who would be coming to Delhi. Seeing him sulk over the oversized baraat, Bhanu joked, 'Don't worry darling, eleven is my lucky number.'

'Mine is thirteen.' Bhushan replied.

'How come thirteen?' Bhanu asked.

'Our Dads are also coming.'

~

The baraat, or the 'Dirty 11' as Bhanu had named the contingent, reached Gangtok just as dusk settled over the quaint town. There was a mild chill in the crisp evening air, and the sky was awash with many hues of orange. A small group, led by Buddy, welcomed the baraatis at the station and drove them to their hotel. After checking in and freshening up, they headed for the Bhutia home. Bhanu and her mother led the neighbourhood in receiving them with a traditional tilak. As soon as they were settled, butter tea, the traditional welcome brew, was served in pretty dragon bowls along with snacks. There were momos, home-baked confectionaries, egg bhujias and steamy pakoras.

Handing out the plates, Buddy's mother said, 'Please have some light snacks. Later, we will have a full dinner at our home.'

The snacking was more than a hearty meal. Being against food wastage, Bhanu's mother politely refused the invitation, 'This is more than a full dinner! And it is late evening, so please don't bother with dinner.'

Hearty snacking was followed by hearty chatter, and it went on until midnight before everyone retired to their rooms.

The next morning, Bhanu arranged for an impromptu mehndi ceremony at her home. She had done it more as a fun activity than a custom, so the invitation was not limited to ladies. She Whatsapped her Gangtok gang, 'Hello hello, surprise! Have arranged a snap mehndi ceremony for my upcoming marriage. Everyone's invited. 7-ish, my place. P.S. Bring your own mehndi. Food and fun will be on me.'

Then she called her man Friday, 'Wake up, my friend-in-need, help is required urgently.'

Buddy replied, 'Yes I saw your message. What all do we need for the ceremony?'

Bhanu referred to her list, 'Refreshments and snacks, simple meal, flowers to deck up the place. And oh, know of a dholi and shehnai player for a live cacophony? Failing which, some loud, raunchy music. And yeah, some mehndi too. Now move your butt, Budds.'

And Buddy did just that.

By 7:30 in the evening, the Bhutias' house was packed to capacity. The young brigade was present in full force, and so teasing and flirting were the order of the evening. Buddy had managed to gather some mehndi cones, but getting hold of a mehndi artist in Gangtok was impossible, so two girls who were good at freehand drawing doubled up as mehndi experts.

As the evening progressed, the young crowd came into its own. People danced the bhangra and disco on the same music simultaneously. Boys jived with the girls and they reciprocated. However, the epicentre of attraction was Bhushan's Mausi, the unrelenting inclusion in the baraat. Clad in a heavily embroidered sari and laden with kilos of gold, she started jiving to a high-energy Bollywood wedding song. Someone from the young brigade whispered, 'Jewellery ka mobile showroom.'

Someone else replied, 'Arre no, this is Zaveri Bazaar on wheels.'

As the song picked up tempo, Mausi became hyper. The boys whistled and the girls cheered, and that was like offering Rum to a monkey. As the song ended on a high, her body wasn't able to take the strain and came down crashing on the floor. There was shocked silence; then Bhushan's mother ran toward her sister, crying, 'What happened????'

'An earthquake, that's what happened' Someone from the Gangtok gang filled in, and suppressed giggles followed.

Bhushan's mother had Mausi's face in her lap and was frantically sprinkling water on it. After a few splashes, Mausi opened her eyes and looked at her sister uncomprehendingly. Bhushan's mother asked her, 'Are you okay, sister?'

Sitting up with help from three persons, Mausi replied, 'Yes, better now. Just felt a little bit dizzy.'

The mishap mellowed the festive mood for a while, but it picked up after refreshments. The party got divided into the young and the young-at-heart, and merriment went on till late night.

May 4—D Day!

Bhanu was awake by five. She messaged Bhushan.

—Your last day as Bhushan Bhanu Pratap Singh.

—Why so?

—Tomorrow, you'll be renamed Bhushan Bhutia.

—Ha! How about you becoming Bhanu Bhutia Singh?

—Will let you know.

A small family gathering was arranged at ten at the Bhutia's home to exchange goodwill gifts; lavish gifting was mutually done away with. First, Bhanu's mother stood up. She handed the flaming red sari and the ring to the bride and the groom, as Dr Bhutia had asked. It was an emotional moment, but she handled it with dignity. As she handed Bhanu the sari, she said, 'Thanks, Mum, and Dad, this is your legacy gift. I will always be proud of it.'

Then she gave the ring to Bhushan. He slipped it in his finger and said, 'Perfect fit.'

'Just as you two are,' Bhanu's mother said fondly.

That done, she took out two pretty gift boxes and quietly slipped one each in Bhushan and Bhanu's palms, saying, 'This is from your mother.'

Bhanu's box contained a beautiful, slim platinum necklace with a winged heart pendant and Bhushan's gift was a Cartier watch, a round, black-and-grey model. He liked it immediately, 'So, I am the timekeeper to the family.'

'You are the keeper of the family now.' Bhanu's mother replied.

Bhushan's mother was next to stand up. She had hand-picked five dresses, five saris, the ceremonial wedding outfit and some jewellery for Bhanu. Gripping Bhanu in a bear hug before giving away the gifts, she said, 'I always longed for a daughter, and now God has given me one.'

Bhanu replied warmly, 'With you around Mummy, I won't miss Maa too much.'

Then she unwrapped the beautiful ancestral bracelet from a silk pouch, the one she had to sell during their worst days. She put it in Bhanu's hands, 'This bracelet has kept the family united through good times and bad, for generations, beti. I am so proud to now pass it on to you. Welcome to the Singh family.'

Bhanu marvelled at the intricately carved bracelet and said, 'Mummy ji, I will treasure this gift and never let the Singh family down.'

Bhushan's mother was about to succumb to tears, so Bhushan quickly intervened, 'Enough of pestering the bride, Mummy. Where is my gift?'

Mother's plump face glowed like a full moon, and she took her son in a long, emotional embrace, 'Live long, my son. For you, I've selected this.'

It was a heavy men's bracelet in gold, studded with four rubies along its length. Bhushan took it in his hands and pretended to stumble under its weight, 'It's too heavy!'

And mother laughed at that, 'You're a married man now, learn to bear the weight.'

Bhanu got up to make an unexpected announcement, 'Ehm ehm, we—Bhushan and I would also like to give you all a small gift to make this evening memorable.'

Everybody was surprised. They had never received a gift from a bride and groom in a wedding and were perturbed at the gesture. Bhanu opened a box of 3 oz bottles of *Premier Amour* perfume and started giving one to everyone. As a few impatient ones tried out the perfume on the back of their palms, the exotic tuberose scent filled the air.

First love was all over the room.

~

Around two in the noon, Bhushan received a message from Brinda, 'Many congratulations! May the Almighty shower His choicest blessings on the couple of the decade! Best wishes for a happy and blissful matrimonial journey—Brinda.'

Bhushan was deeply moved—He thought, what magnanimity, what large-heartedness, what a sterling character this lady possesses! He replied instantly, 'Can I call you?'

Brinda typed back, 'Why not, are we enemies?'

When she answered his call, he said, 'Brinda! I would have known it was you even if you had not put your name to it.'

'How so?'

'I don't know anyone else with such a big, forgiving heart.'

'Who am I to forgive Bhush, err, Bhushan?' Brinda questioned him, 'Besides, it's not like me to hold grudges. Please convey my wishes to Bhanu as well.'

Bhushan said, 'Sure I will.' Then he added, 'Err, I wish I had not come in your life and caused you so much suffering. I am sorry, I really am.'

'It's okay. Had you not come in my life, I would have never learned to love. And the suffering has ended, or rather, turned into bittersweet memories, thanks mostly to Baldev.'

'Baldev? Do you mean Buddy? How?' Bhushan was surprised, confused, totally at a loss.

'Yes Bhushan, Baldev—Dev for me. He and I have bonded.'

The news was a bolt out of the blue. Bhushan was disbelieving at first, and when the words sank in, elated. He was so overwhelmed. He could not respond immediately.

'Won't you congratulate me?' Brinda quipped, 'Lol, I am fishing for compliments.'

Bhushan, 'You gave me shock treatment, lol. Brinda, you can't imagine how glad I am for you, for both of you.' His mind instantly pictured a happy portrait of her with Buddy, and he could not help marvelling at it, 'Wow what a couple!'

With joy, came relief. Bhushan felt a heavy weight being lifted from his heart. *Whatever I had done to Brinda, has been undone by destiny*, he thought, *Buddy will keep her very happy, and she will fill his life with bliss and contentment.*

With that sense of redemption, he could say what he felt, 'My heartiest congratulations Brinda, I am speechless with joy, really! You pulled off a major one! What a great catch! Now I know a huge conspiracy was being hatched behind my back.'

Then curiosity got better of him, 'Tell me the how and where and when of it! I'm dying to know.'

And so Brinda told him how her first encounter with Buddy at the launch of FRA was a comedy of error. Their Whatsapp chats became a daily routine after Brinda sent Buddy their selfie. How their friendship had culminated in an easy and smoothly flowing, uncomplicated love built on Brinda's amiable nature and Buddy's mountain-people naiveté and nobility. How Baldev had become Dev for her, and how his dream girl Rasmi had stepped out of the posters in his room to enter his real life. How their love thrived on virtue and like-mindedness as much as on looks and attraction.

Bhushan was fascinated, 'Whoa! What a love story! You're a winsome couple.'

She said, 'Yes, Bhushan, I am happy. Ours is a relationship low on demands and high on deliverance.'

'How true!' he said, 'So when is "the couple of the decade" tying the knot?'

'On 24 June. The preparations are on. Although the formal invitation will be sent later—you, I mean, Bhanu and you, will attend.'

It was obvious from the way she said it, that she needed him to be there while she was marrying someone else.

He promised her, 'I—we will be there.'

He punched Bhanu's number immediately after the call ended.

'There is news.'

'That your bride-to-be eloped?'

'Ha! Something far more scandalous.'

'What?'

'Hold your breath.'

'Okay, holding.'

'Brinda and Buddy are getting married in late June.' He announced dramatically as he entered Bhanu's room.

'Ffffuucccckkk no!' Bhanu screamed, her disbelief latching on to the F-factor for a full ten seconds. When she could think of something else, she blurted, 'This is fuckingly unbelievable or vice-versa, Bhushy! You mean it?'

'I can't be more serious.'

'Well, well, well...' She was still at a loss of words, but within her, a giant wave of happiness for Brinda had started rising. As for Buddy, she thought the Almighty had finally blessed him.

'This is seriously great news, Bhushy. Even as we talk, I am sending out my prayers to Brinda and Buddy.'

They talked some more about the incredibility of this major coup, when the antique clock in Bhanu's room struck 3:00 p.m., she said, 'Okay, well, great news but bad timing. I was just starting to get ready to marry you. See ya at the marriage mandap—gallows for you in three hours.'

The moment Bhushan was gone, she went looking for Buddy. He was helping with the decoration at the far end of the veranda.

'Dev!'

Bhanu yelled and ran toward Buddy.

Buddy was caught totally off-guard. Who would call him by that name here? He turned around and saw Bhanu rushing toward him like a driver-less engine. She threw him off-balance with her energy as she hugged him. Letting him go only after she was satisfied that she had hugged him enough, she launched her barrage, 'Cunning, conspiring bastard! You managed to keep it a secret from me! How dare you!'

Buddy realized what it was about. He smiled impishly. Then, blushing from ear to ear, he offered a lame explanation, 'We have not told anyone.'

'So, I am "anyone" for you, huh?'

'No, no, I was going to tell you as soon as you were free.'

'You can do better than that Budds.'

Then he became candid, 'Okay Bhanu, seriously, my parents are a little conservative. They will take some time to accept my marriage outside our community. That's why I was a bit hesitant to tell you.'

'Oh, that!' Bhanu shrugged it off, 'No worries, Budds, I am a double-PhD in dealing with unwilling parents. I will talk to them.'

'Okay,' Buddy said. However, he could not hold back his curiosity, 'By the way, how did you come to know?'

She told him about Brinda's call to Bhushan, 'That's how we came to know.'

Holding him by his arms, her face a mask of pride and joy,

she added, 'Damn, I am so soo happy Buddy! It's the news of the decade, and Brinda and you are the couple of the century!'

'Thank you sooo much, Bhanu, and you are coming to the wedding.'

'Of course, but first, let me take care of mine.'

Pinching Buddy's cheeks, she breezed out.

~

Bhanu was dressed in the traditional Bhutia bridal attire for the wedding, while Bhushan had selected a royal sherwani and a headgear with a feathered crest. He looked dashing and handsome in his two-day-old stubble.

By six, the groom's party reached the wedding venue and after a brief reception, the bride and groom garlanded each other. The groom was led to the marriage pandal decorated with marigold flowers. Soon thereafter, Buddy's father, who also performed the Kanyadaan rite, led the bride to the platform. When Bhushan took Bhanu's hand in his for the panigrahana ritual, he vowed, 'I take this oath in the presence of the celestial powers and the agni devta to be your protector and provider.'

The ritual of saptapadi or the seven vows is a transformational rite wherein a couple reckons and accepts the higher responsibilities of virtuous domesticity. As Bhushan and Bhanu circled around the sacred fire seven times, they could feel the transformation occurring in them.

After that, Bhushan tied the mangal sutra around Bhanu's neck and whispered in her ears, 'Congratulations, Mrs Bhanu Singh.'

Bhanu smiled and whispered back, 'To you too, Mr Bhushan Bhutia.'

After the rituals, both the families assembled to remember

Bhanu Pratap Singh and Dr Bhutia. A combined photograph of both of them sat on a table in a room. It was an edited picture. The two gentlemen had never met but their portraits were photoshopped in such a way that they looked like old buddies. They were all smiles, as if they had just reunited after ages.

First, Bhushan's mother paid her tribute. Her lips fluttered as she prayed silently, tears forming at the corners of her tightly shut eyes. Then, Bhanu's mother came forward and stood before the photo in stoic silence. After a minute, she motioned to Bhanu and Bhushan and said, 'Come, seek their blessings. They are here only briefly.'

The couple stepped forward. Bhanu's eyes fogged as she looked at the photo, but Bhushan squeezed her shoulder gently. The emotional moment passed. Bhanu smiled and said to her Paa, 'My Daddy strongest; always be around in our lives like a guardian angel.'

Then Bhushan said to his father, 'Superman, I promise to walk on your path and be a responsible husband and father.'

Finally, it was time for bidaai. Hearts started wallowing. No daughter on earth can migrate to womanhood without a momentary sense of loss of daughterhood. However, there were no emotional overtures. A long, pining hug, and her mother holding Bhanu by her shoulders and saying, 'Go, make me proud' was all that transpired between mother and daughter before she stepped out of maidenhood.

~

The first night!

Bhanu's room was decorated sparingly with a few marigold strings tied in an arch on the poles of the large teakwood bed.

The customary glass of milk and dry fruits were missing on the side table, on Bhanu's instructions. She was certain her sex-starved husband was not going to need those supplements.

'Sturdy bed,' Bhushan said as he jumped on it.

'Will stand tonight's test,' she replied.

Then mischief seized her. She quickly changed her expressions to become the virgin bride and moved a few inches away from Bhushan, 'My brand-new husband, show some chivalry. Would you lift my veil?'

Bhushan stopped her mid-way, 'Oye, drama queen, you weren't shy even on what was actually our first night.'

'It was day then,' she corrected him and asked, 'Husband dear, what do couples do conventionally on their wedding night?'

'They screw.'

'How very eloquent!' Bhanu rolled her eyes in a taunt, 'So let's be unconventional and let's not screw tonight.'

'Unacceptable!' Bhushan jumped in protest, 'We've not met for 21 days and I'm starved for sex.'

Then, to press his protest further, he repeated in chaste Hindi, 'यौन क्रीडा का मेरा आज इक्कीसवा उपवास है।'

Bhanu doubled up laughing, barely managing some winks in-between.

When she had regained her breath, Bhushan leaned and kissed her gently. She responded instantly and pulled him to her, rubbing her cheeks on his stubble. The roughness stoked raw desire in her, 'Sleazy bastard, you're smoking hot tonight.'

'Beware, you're playing with fire.'

Bhanu let out low, husky laughter and said, 'WTF, let's make lava-hot love.'

Around pre-dawn, the couple lay spent in each other's arms, sleeping like tangled creepers on a windless night.

16

The End Is a New Beginning

Zanskar in summer is a transformed place. The predominating white of the winter is replaced by many hues of temperate nature—the frigid ecology springs to life with the warmth of the season. The air gets laden with the heavy scent of wild poppies and pink Balsam. The melting snow exposes the brownish-grey skin of the hills and mountains. The sky flirts with many hues of blue and the clouds rush past it like nomads going nowhere. The pristine lakes and ponds mirror the sky so truly that one cannot make out which is the reflection. The yaks and the horses and the herdsmen all have fantastic outings. The meadows look like unkempt golf courses. The colourful prayer flags adorning the tiny stone shrines flutter wildly in the wind as if to liberate the chants inscribed on them. And the chants seem impatient too, to disperse in the air and bless the elements.

And oh, the River Zanskar! From a snow anaconda in hibernation, it springs to life with the tremendous force of young waters freshly released from the bondage of snow. Like a woman mad in love, it gushes brusquely on its course. Around the turn of the Nerak Bridge, it becomes frantic, as if its long-lost lover was finally in sight. Quite in contrast with the eerie, deathly silence of winter, the atmosphere around the Nerak Bridge comes alive with the full-throated roars of the River.

It is here that Bhanu and Bhushan had chosen to camp for their honeymoon. That was the place that had separated them, and that is where they would unite permanently.

The couple had so much to do on their honeymoon. They would join a group of rafters and explore the Zanskar River's vivacious, erratic moods or roam the wild, virgin expanses at whim. They would pretend to know the language of the rustling leaves and the whistling winds and talk to them in gibberish. They would lie on the grass and invent crazy names for the passing clouds. They would make wildflower bouquets for each other. Bhanu would sing love songs for Bhushan in her lovely voice and he would pluck passion fruit for her. They would make love randomly and primitively, in the open or behind a bush or beneath a rocky ledge, without prescribed niceties. Afterwards, they would collect deadwood for that evening's campfire.

Toward dusk, they would regroup with the rafters on the riverbank. The group leader played wonderful guitar so there would be a lot of singing and storytelling until the evening mellowed. Then they would head for their tent perched on a clearing over the riverbank.

~

On the last night of their honeymoon, Bhanu and Bhushan lay on their backs in the tent holding hands. They had just made sweet, unhurried emotional love.

'How was it?' He asked her habitually.

'Like thanksgiving to Zanskar.'

It was a clear full moon night, so the stars did not seem very bright or low. Bhanu demanded, 'Hey hubby, pluck some fresh, ripe stars for me.'

'Not tonight,' replied Bhushan, 'They are overpowered by the moon.'

'Then get me the moon.'

And Bhushan did something which Bhanu would never forget in her life. He reached out to the moon with outstretched hands, cupped it in his palms, and gently put it on Bhanu's tummy. Then he said, 'Our first child, whenever it graces our lives, will be like the moon tonight. Whether Bunty or Babli, it will have a fully radiant persona, not only glowing itself but also illuminating its surroundings. Bhanu, my sun, you will bear such a full moon for us.'

Bhanu cried, and Bhushan cuddled her like a child. On their last night in Zanskar, they became complete as man and wife. They learned their final lesson on how to love and live from Zanskar—by giving and sharing everything unconditionally.

Later that day, Bhanu and Bhushan visited Nerak village. Since the snow had melted, it had become much easier to approach the village. Memories invaded them as they reached the village, but both had determined not to let the past play a spoilsport.

As they entered the village, a passer-by stopped, looked at them, then looked again with squinted eyes, and his face creased into a broad grin as he recognized Bhanu. He was one of the villagers who had carried Bhanu on the stretcher to Nerak Bridge. He asked her in broken English, 'Memshaab you, here?'

Bhanu greeted him, 'Juley! Yes, it's me.'

The villager bobbed his head and said, 'I am sho happy to shee you.' Then he gave a side glance to Bhushan and continued, 'Err, you both, here, again?'

Bhanu sought to put his curiosity at rest, 'We had some problems that are now over. We just got married and are here in Zanskar for our honeymoon. We thought of visiting you all and saying thank you for your help last time.'

'No no, not thank you to us, we only did our duty'

Then the villager asked their names.

'I am Bhanu and he is Bhushan.'

He bobbed his head and grinned broadly, 'I am very happy to meet you both.'

Then, just like that, he invited them to his home, 'Come have shome tea.'

Bhanu and Bhushan accepted readily. Then, just like that, the villager also offered food, 'Memshaab, Shaab, come for lunsch alsho with tea.'

How could they refuse such a heartfelt invitation?

The villager was overjoyed. He called his son who was playing in the open ground and asked him to run home and inform mother about the guests. The child smiled from ear to ear and sprinted towards home.

When they reached the villager's home—a bare, single-room mud-and-brick dwelling, the family of five was beaming with pride at being the host of the 'celebrity foreigners.' The homemaker lady greeted Bhanu and Bhushan with a jovial 'juleyy' and spread a quilt for them on the floor. She quickly poured butter tea boiling on a wood-fire stove and offered it to them. After tea, they came out in the open and sat on a wooden plank resting on two tree barks. Lunch was served after some time—Zanskari 'papa' made of barley flour, butter and peas, and 'mok-mok', a native variety of ravioli. They ate heartily while talking to the family.

Around three, Bhanu and Bhushan got ready to leave.

'One minute,' the gentleman said. His wife opened a rickety trunk and brought out a hand-woven stole.

'Gift,' she beamed at Bhanu and Bhushan.

Bhanu melted, overwhelmed by the gesture. Of course the turquoise blue stole was exquisite and beautiful, but more than the stole, it was the magnanimity of her hostess that stole her heart. She hugged the lady warmly and said, 'Thank you! It is so beautiful!'

She then looked at Bhushan questioningly, as if to ask, 'What shall we give them?'

On an impulse, Bhushan took out his sports watch that had many outdoor features useful for the mountain people. He put it in the gentleman's palms.

The villager was taken aback; he knew it was an expensive watch, 'No, no, shaab, I can't take it.' But Bhushan insisted. He patted his back, 'Keep it.'

The entire village had flocked to bid them adieu. Bhanu and Bhushan kept waving until their arms hurt.

On their way back, they halted at the plateau where they had separated. Bhanu said a bit wryly, 'The Break-up Point.'

Bhushan replied, 'It is hereby renamed as The Bonding Point.'

Unmindful of the on-looking villagers, they hugged for a long time, standing motionless in each other's arms, their breathing hardly palpable. When they broke the hug, Bhushan said, 'Until death does us apart.'

'Not even then,' Bhanu murmured.

~

The next morning, they were ready to leave by ten. Bhanu took several deep breaths, trying to fill her lungs with as much mountain air as possible. Her gaze travelled as far as the sweeping mountains and beyond, where the skyscrapers became one with the sky. She turned back and looked at the towering rocky ledge behind her, then to her right at the melted icefall and to her left at the Bridge. At last, she looked below at the gushing river. A strange thought crossed her mind. She compared her mental state with that of a bride leaving her maternal home, and suddenly, Zanskar became that home to her. The mountains seemed like a protective father, the fertile river below, a giving mother. The ledge behind her seemed like a watchful aunt and the waterfall, like a vivacious younger sibling.

Bhanu had withheld from crying at the time of her bidaai, but she shed her restraint while bidding adieu to Zanskar, the home that had taught her how to love and live rightly.

After many minutes of reverie, Bhanu stepped out of her newfound home with a heavy heart.

'The end,' she told Bhushan.

'The beginning,' he replied and took her hand in his, guiding her to their shared future.

∽

Epilogue

The Brinda-Buddy wedding in Delhi was a 'proper' one, as Bhushan's mother put it. It was a four-day-long event, with a sangeet, mehndi ceremony, wedding and reception spread across four days of non-stop merriment and food fiesta. Bhushan had shouldered the responsibility of all proceedings for Buddy's, and Bhanu was a willing accomplice. The wedding had given Bhushan's mother a chance to splurge wealth on Brinda, which was denied to her earlier. She shopped and shopped, calling Brinda ten times a day whether she would like purple for this sari, or ochre for that dress, or to ask whether she preferred a choker necklace in pearls or studs. Her fondness for Brinda found outlets at shops all over Delhi. She still doted over her.

Buddy's father and mother had blessed the alliance wholeheartedly after Bhanu spoke to them. Enjoying the limelight as the groom's parents, they beamed all the time. Brinda went out of her way to put them at ease in the affluent surroundings. She made it a point to introduce them to guests, which were so many that they would mix them up. Buddy's mother mistook Laxmi bhua for Rashmi fufi, and Brinda made light of it, saying, 'Mummyji, it's okay, mix-ups happen. It is due to a mix-up that Dev and I bonded. So chill!'

'Chill?' Mummy asked.

Brinda laughed. 'Chill means to take it easy.'

As for Bhanu and Bhushan, it was redemption time. At the

end of the festivities, when Buddy got emotional and started thanking them for shouldering the burden of a lavish marriage, Bhanu put her finger on her lips and patted his face affectionately, 'Ssshhh, Buddy, no thank-yous. It's a godsend opportunity to give back what you have done for us.'

And Brinda and Baldev—Devi and Dev, as Bhanu had renamed them, were happy, very happy. Like Bhanu and Bhushan, they too dreamed of having their own kids. They would name them Roshni and Chirag. Their light would illuminate their happy home each evening.

༄

A Parting Note

Dear reader,

Thank you for reading our love story. You will be glad to know, FRA, the wonderland of French fragrances is doing well. And hurray! Bhushan is not frigid! Bunty or Babli, is on the way and should be here in the next sixty to seventy days. We are excited and nervous. And we are happy. Never thought such happiness existed. But it does, and to experience it is to experience lasting true love. It is pure bliss, to be in love and raise a family with the one you love. And if it's *premier amour*—first love, the feeling is ten times more blissful.

We want to tell something to the lovers' fraternity, and that's why this short note before we take your leave.

Zanskar is the womb of our love. It has taught us that if you have loved truly, it's for keeps, as the bonding between the timeless snow and the ancient, lofty mountains. But we weaken that bond with our base human tendencies. Actually, love never fails us, we fail love. We fall into the trappings of deceit, doubt and prejudgment and screw it up. Fortunately, Almighty A. Altruist offered us a second chance. What if He wouldn't have? To love and to lose in love is worse than not to love.

Many of you would have been newly in love when you read our story. To them, we want to say that true love is a rare lucky charm. Always wear it close to your heart. Treasure it and value its boundless worth. It will open the doors to a magical world that not everybody is blessed to experience. Good luck, going forward.

Some of you would be seasoned lovers passing through your mid-love lives when you leafed through these pages. We are sure you would have graduated from entry-level kissing and achieved proficiency in that core skill. But while at it, also focus on developing the soft skills as lovers. Be as understanding and accommodating toward each other as possible, especially toward each other's weaknesses. Agreed, each one of us has different threshold levels, but don't blow the lid in a hurry. Shared life is about sharing one's personal space. It is not intrusion, it is inclusion. Moral of the story: fairy tales don't happen just like that. Don't believe that crap. Lovers have to work toward making them happen.

And lastly, a few of you (as few as possible, God, please) would be facing a break-up while reading our story. Don't take it lying down. Although it's better said than done (who knows that better than us?), if you think what you let slip past your fingers was true love, fight back fiercely to regain lost ground. Consider it a life-and-death situation, for it is. Don't just drown yourself in tears of self-pity. Get up, gather your guts and wits, and travel your part of the distance to meet them halfway. When you are there, be the first to extend the hand; a hug is even better if circumstances permit. Then speak your heart out to clear the misgivings. Don't let that knot in your throat mute your voice. There may not be another day, another chance. So, seize the moment. Be born-again lovers and rediscover the magic of true love.

Friends, from Zanskar to Gangtok to Cannes, then back to Gangtok and Zanskar for honeymoon, and now finally, to Delhi, the journey has been like one of those high-adrenaline theme park rides. The highs and lows have only strengthened our love for each other. Why so? Because no matter what, we believe in love like one believes in his faith and religion.

So that's it. Before we say goodbye, all you lovers out there, chant with us,

Let's ride the tide.

Love is by our side.

Signing off now, with lots of love,
Bhanu and Bhushan

Gratitude

This novel found its roots in the pristine, man-made paradise at Jain Hills, Jalgaon, which today serves as the headquarters of Jain Irrigation Systems. One man, the late Dr Bhavarlal H. Jain (Bhau), a Padma Shri awardee, created bliss amidst this arid wasteland. Here, he walked the talk, 'Leave the world better than you found it.' I bow to this man and the vibes of Jain Hills.

My sincere thanks and deep appreciation to Sandhya Chandrasekharayya and Ezhil Suresh—your invaluable insights on Zanskar and the Chadar Trek helped me build the narrative.

And large-hearted gratitude to my friends—your stubborn belief in me is always an inspiration.

12 December 2011, at Jain Hills, Jalgaon, with the late Dr Bhavarlal H. Jain (Bhau), a Padma Shri awardee and founder and former chairman of Jain Irrigation Systems Limited. It was there that this love story took roots.